Call Me Margo

Call Me Margo

Judith St. George

G.P. Putnam's Sons / New York

Library of Congress Cataloging in Publication Data
St. George, Judith.
    Call me Margo.
    Summary: In yet another new school, a shy 15-year-old
has difficulty adjusting to her first boarding school,
especially since the tennis team is hostile toward her.
    [1. Boarding schools—Fiction.   2. School stories.
3. Tennis—Fiction.   4. Bashfulness—Fiction]   I. Title.
PZ7.S142Cal   [Fic]   80-29532
ISBN 0-399-20790-2

To my friend Patricia Gauch

Call Me Margo

one

BZZZZZ.

The buzzer sounded right outside Margo's room. Since it was just six o'clock, she figured it must be the buzzer for dinner. Sure enough, doors opened and closed all up and down the hall. First, Margo heard voices and footsteps approaching, then she saw the girls pass her room, two together, three together, even clusters of four or five, all talking and some of them even laughing. None of them were alone. Like Margo. Well, she'd just stay in her room where she was. There was no way she was going down into that big dining room by herself.

Then the last of the stragglers was gone and the clatter of their feet on the bare stairs had faded away, too. The whole third floor was silent. Terribly silent. Still Margo stood by her window staring out. A 747 jet etched a thin white line high over the rooftops and she wondered if that was the plane she had arrived on, now on its way back to Los Angeles. All of a sudden, Margo wished she were on it. She sighed a deep sigh, fighting back the tears. It had been a long day. She had flown all the way from Los Angeles to Philadelphia and then driven from the airport in the school van here to the Haywood School.

The Haywood School. Margo had counted on Haywood to be different, but it wasn't different at all. Because her family had moved around so much, Margo had never lived anywhere long enough to feel really settled. Now that she was fifteen and a sophomore, she had been looking forward to boarding school and staying in the same place for three straight years and making the first real friends of her life. But as soon as Margo had arrived, she'd found out that both her roommates were juniors and had already been at Haywood for two years. As old girls they wouldn't even be arriving for three days.

As Margo watched the jet vapor wiggle, blur, then disappear, her stomach growled and she realized she hadn't eaten since breakfast and that was Los Angeles time, which was three hours later than Philadelphia time. Or was it three hours earlier? It didn't matter. She would never survive without food until tomorrow. She'd just have to go into that dining room alone whether she wanted to or not.

Margo went downstairs and peered around the

open dining room doors. Three-fourths of the long room was empty, with all the chairs piled on top of the tables. But at the far end, a couple of big tables were filled with girls all chattering like a flock of high-pitched birds. The clink of their silver and glasses echoed the length of the room. Like Margo, these were the new girls who had arrived early for orientation. But by the way they were jabbering, Margo guessed a whole lot of them must have known each other before today.

Luckily, Margo had changed into sneakers so she didn't make a sound as she headed toward the tables. So far, so good. No one had noticed her. She'd just get a tray and sit down at the table nearest the kitchen where she had already spotted an empty place. She had just picked up a tray to get her food when someone on the other side of the room let out a yell.

"Hey, you, Martha, from the third floor. C'mon over and sit with us."

Instinctively, Margo turned around, but there was no one behind her who could possibly be Martha. The girl must have meant her. Margo had seen the girl before. It would be hard to miss her. She had long straight black hair and she was at least six feet tall. Now she was waving to Margo. Oh no, everyone in the dining room had turned around to look. Margo felt herself blush as she quickly filled her tray with food.

The only empty chair at the table was next to the tall girl. Margo slid into it as unobtrusively as possible.

"Hi, Martha," the tall girl greeted her.

Before Margo could correct her, the tall girl had

turned to the person next to her, a funny looking little blond with a quizzical monkey face and an afro of tight curls. The two of them were discussing something as if they'd known each other forever. Everyone else was busy talking too, mostly, it seemed, about teachers and classes. Grateful that nothing was expected of her, Margo started eating.

One fat girl covered with freckles seemed to know everything. "My sister said if you get Mr. O'Brien after lunch, he sleeps through most of the period. He's a gravy grader too, nothing lower than a C."

The tall girl jumped right into the conversation. "What about Mrs. Maglione? I have her for English and it's my worst subject."

"Maglione's the best. I requested her when I applied," the fat girl answered. "The one to avoid is Durrett. She's a horror and gives terrible grades."

Margo paused with her fork halfway to her mouth. She thought she remembered the name Durrett on her course card, but she wasn't sure. She certainly didn't need that. Even though English was her best subject, she had to work hard just to get average grades. All of a sudden, she didn't feel very hungry.

"How much gym do we have to take?" the little blond with the afro asked.

"Four times a week."

The blond groaned. "Gym is the pits. I begged to go to the Cooper-Morse School because macrame and weaving count as gym but Dad vetoed that."

Everyone laughed. Gym was okay with Margo. Especially tennis.

There was a lull in the conversation and all of a sudden the tall girl stood up and tapped her fork on a glass for quiet. No one paid any attention. She tapped her glass again. Though a few of the girls looked up, it wasn't until she hit her glass for the third time that the thirty or forty girls in the room quieted down.

"Since we're all new here I think we should get to know each other," she began in a booming voice. "First of all, let's find out who's what, you know, like freshmen or sophomores or whatever. Raise your hand if you're a freshman."

Most of the hands went up. Only 8 or 10 were left.

"Okay, who's a sophomore?"

As Margo raised her hand, she noticed that both the tall girl and the blond next to her raised their hands along with two other girls. She also noticed that a couple of the older girls were rolling their eyes at each other with who-does-she-think-she-is expressions.

"What about juniors?"

The last three hands went up reluctantly. They belonged to the three girls who had exchanged disgusted glances. One of them was the fat girl whose sister had gone to Haywood.

The tall girl was still standing. "Now I think we should go around the room and give our names so we can get to know each other. My name is Jill Strennett, though everyone has called me Stretch since fourth grade—for what reason I can't imagine, especially since I'm still growing." She laughed and so did some of the younger girls. Margo's laugh was a mixture of admiration for Stretch's nerve and exasperation that Stretch was involving her in something she wanted no part of. It didn't matter. There was no

13

stopping her. Stretch gestured to the blond next to her.

"This is my roommate, Cristina Goodman. Opposites attract and that's us. When they paired us up as roommates, they must have thought Haywood needed a good laugh for the next three years."

The little blond jumped up and raised her hands over her head like a prizefighter. She couldn't have been more than five feet tall. The difference between her height and Stretch's, as well as the contrast between her short blond afro and Stretch's long straight black hair, was so ridiculous that everyone laughed. Neither girl seemed to mind, but Margo felt embarrassed for both of them.

"Hey, a Cristina can't room with a Stretch. How about Cricket?" someone at the next table yelled.

"Yeah, Cricket," another girl chimed in.

Cricket and Stretch. They sounded like freaks in a side show. But apparently, neither of them minded that either. In fact, they seemed pleased.

"I always knew I had a cricket hidden somewhere inside me," Cristina called back.

Stretch held up her hand for silence. "Next to me on the other side is Martha Something-or-other."

Margo was caught by surprise and her face reddened as everyone looked at her.

"My name isn't Martha," she blurted out. "It's Margo Allinger."

"I thought I heard someone call you Martha." Stretch's error didn't seem to bother her. "Where are you from . . ."

"My name is Betsy Hollingshead," the girl on the other side of Margo interrupted so Margo was saved from having to say anything more.

At first Margo tried to remember everyone's name as each girl announced it, but after a while she was so confused by Susies and Sallys and Karens and Kates she gave up. And then they had gone all the way around the room and dinner was over. Margo carried her tray to the kitchen counter along with the rest of the girls. Now they were all breaking up into groups of twos and threes again. Everyone with her roommate, Margo thought, everyone but me.

As Margo left the dining room alone, she realized the three juniors were right behind her. She couldn't help but overhear them.

"I don't believe that performance. I thought Haywood had some kind of standards. How did that girl Stretch ever get accepted?"

"I can't imagine. You'd think she ran the place."

"I was sure she'd have us all playing pin-the-tail-on-the-donkey next. I mean, how childish can you get?"

Margo couldn't understand it either. She felt conspicuous enough just being alone. Why in the world would Stretch attract attention to herself that way by jumping up and taking over? She acted as if she didn't even care what people thought about her. Margo knew she could never do anything like that, not in a million years.

Still shaking their heads and muttering, the three juniors strode past Margo as if they were in a big hurry. They seemed to be friends already. Margo was in no hurry at all. She had nothing to rush for, just an empty echoey room with no one in it but her.

two

Margo's parents were very much on her mind those
first few days alone. They had left Los Angeles the
same day Margo had, only they had flown in the
opposite direction, to the Marshall Islands in the Pa-
cific where Dad, as a consultant, was going to help
the trusteeship of Micronesia set up its own government. He and Mom would be gone for eighteen
months. Eighteen months! It seemed like forever. In
the meantime, it was decided that boarding school
was the best solution for Margo with her married
sister's apartment in New York as a base for vacations.

Luckily, the next two days were so busy Margo didn't have much time to be homesick. Everything was a jumble of names and faces she still couldn't put together, meetings, buying books, taking a physical fitness test, going on a tour of the campus, and buzzers, buzzers, buzzers. The third floor buzzer was right outside her room, and the first couple of times it went off, Margo nearly jumped out of her skin. But after a while, like a rat being conditioned to torture, she got used to it.

The afternoon of the second day, the school held a uniform sale in the front hall. The hall was the most enormous room Margo had ever seen. In fact, the whole boarding part of the school was called Big Hall because of it. A wide staircase led down from the floors above into the cathedral-high room. Ten-foot-long sofas flanked a fireplace large enough to stand in, and carved oak chairs were arranged stiffly around the rest of the room. A formidable grand dame draped with pearls was immortalized in oil over the mantel. The plaque under her portrait was self-explanatory, *Julia Brett Haywood, 1864–1943. Studies Pass into Character.* Margo guessed that Miss Haywood—all determined jawline and grim expression—had probably been full of character.

Big Hall was mass confusion now. All the new girls were milling around half-dressed, snatching uniforms off racks, dropping them on the floor, tossing them to one another. Margo, who was skinny and flat chested, hated to undress in front of anyone so she ducked behind a huge chair to change. She was a size eight, but everyone else must have been a size eight too. She finally settled for a size eight, a six, and a ten.

As Margo got in line to check out, she noticed Stretch standing in front of a mirror trying on a uniform that was about eight inches too short. With her long skinny legs attached to long skinny feet, she looked like an ostrich. Cricket was with her and they were both laughing. As Stretch turned to check her rear view in the mirror, she noticed Margo watching.

"I'm starring in a new movie, Margo," she called over. *"Abraham Lincoln Hits Haywood High."*

"And I can't find a uniform that doesn't drag on the floor," Cricket added with a laugh.

Margo had to laugh too. Those two were something else.

"Name please."

Margo jerked to attention as she realized it was the second time the teacher writing up the charge slips had asked her name.

"Margo Allinger."

The woman looked up. "So you're Margo. Hi, I'm Miss Frye, the tennis coach." She smiled and held out her hand. But Margo's arms were full of uniforms. She quickly put them down and they shook. Miss Frye had a small hand but a strong grip and her brook-blue eyes, a perfect match with her Shetland sweater, crinkled up so little spoke-lines forked out. Her tan looked permanent, the kind that never faded, and she wore her blond hair feathery short.

"Hi, I'm glad to meet you." Margo meant it.

"I'm always on the look-out for good tennis material so I was delighted to see your application." Miss

18

Frye really did seem delighted. "We have a good team. Last year we won the Philadelphia Sectionals and our captain is ranked in the Northeast for eighteen and under. I'll certainly be looking for you at practice on Thursday."

Margo smiled and from the way her face muscles pulled tight, she realized it was probably the first time since she had arrived that she had smiled, really smiled. "I can't wait."

"Good. Three o'clock. Right after Eighth period."

Going to bed in that dreary room with its yawning curtainless windows was the worst part of not having a roommate, but that night Margo felt better. Miss Frye had seemed genuinely glad to meet her. It was funny. Tennis was the one thing in Margo's life she had confidence in. Once she stepped out on that tennis court, a surge of adrenaline or self-assurance or something made her feel good about herself. Haywood's strong tennis program was one of the main reasons she had picked Haywood when she and her mother had toured boarding schools last spring. Most of the schools she had attended hadn't done much with tennis, except for the one in California last year. But she had always found community courts or indoor courts to rent, and if there wasn't anyone to play with, her father would always give her a workout. In lots of ways, tennis was the glue that held her together.

Margo stared up at the shadows on her ceiling. Now that she had met Miss Frye, things were looking up. She liked Miss Frye and Miss Frye seemed to like her, and Thursday she would meet the rest of the team. Those were the girls who would be her friends.

And tomorrow when her roommates arrived, she wouldn't have to sleep alone in this gloomy, empty room again. All of a sudden, Margo sensed that maybe Haywood was going to work out for her after all.

three

There wasn't much planned for the next day. The school was geared up for the old girls' arrival, checking them in, registering them for classes and staging a secondhand furniture sale. Margo hung around the front hall most of the morning waiting for her roommate. She already knew her name, Eva Gordon.

Last August when Haywood had sent her Eva's name and address, Margo had written to her. When Eva hadn't answered, Margo figured she was probably on vacation and hadn't received it. Now that she knew Eva had already been at Haywood two years and was a junior, she hoped her letter had never arrived. It was all about how Margo had spent her life moving around the country and how she couldn't wait to go to boarding school and stay in one place for three years, even though she was scared to death. At least the two of them could face the first day terrors together. Looking back on what she had written, she realized how childish she must have sounded.

Beth Jo McIver was the name of Margo's other roommate, though someone told Margo that everyone called her B.J. Actually, B.J. was Margo's suite mate. Because Haywood had once been an old hotel, the rooms were divided up into suites with combinations of doubles and singles. Number 36, Margo's suite, consisted of a double room for Eva and Margo, and a single for B.J., with a bathroom separating the two rooms.

Margo was checking her mailbox by the main desk, which she knew was a waste of time because it was too soon for any mail to arrive, when she heard a squeal behind her. "Eva!"

Margo didn't know who screamed it, but it was the name she had been waiting for. She edged over to the corner of the mailboxes and peered around. Not twenty-five feet away, two girls raced toward each other with their arms out. A tall, good-looking woman and a young blond man stood nearby, surrounded by luggage and cartons.

"B.J., you are the greatest," the taller of the two girls exclaimed. "You look even more fantastic than last year."

"Jes' plain ol' Beth Jo McIver, that's me," the other girl answered. Then she turned to the woman and

22

they hugged and exchanged kisses in the air. "Hi, Mrs. Cutler. It's good to see you."

"Dear, you grow more glamorous every year. I'm insanely jealous." The woman smiled, then waved in the direction of the young man. "I'd like you to meet my husband, Doug Cutler, B.J. Doug, this is B.J. McIver, Eva's dearest friend."

Though the young man Doug smiled as they shook hands, he was obviously bored. "Glad to meet you," he murmured.

"Hey, let's get upstairs. I can't wait to tell you about my summer," Eva said as she handed two suitcases to the young man. B.J. picked up a duffel bag, two shopping bags full-to-bursting, a saddle, and the whole troupe started up the stairs.

It was dumb. Margo knew that. She should have just walked up and told them who she was. But she couldn't. A terrible shyness had gripped her. She felt like an intruder just listening to their conversation, let alone interrupting it. She watched them head up the stairs, their footsteps clattering on the bare wood, and she couldn't help gawking. She even had to make a conscious effort to close her mouth. B.J. McIver was beautiful. She wasn't cute or pretty or good-looking. She was outrageously beautiful. She had long blond hair pulled back in an untidy ponytail and heavy dark eyebrows over dark, almost black eyes. Her skin was fair, bordering on pale, and her nose was straight and perfect. It didn't matter that she wore beat-up jeans, an old ripped sweater, rubber flip-flops and shuffled along in a careless kind of slouch. She was stunning.

Margo was so struck by B.J. she didn't pay much attention to Eva, except to notice that she wasn't really pretty or not-pretty. She was just average-looking with shiny long dark hair, a not-very-good complexion and washed-out blue eyes that sort of bulged. Then as Margo watched the group walk across the stair landing, she realized that Eva had on a terrific-looking blazer and skirt that were straight out of an advertisement captioned, *For your arrival at that special boarding school.*

Margo swallowed hard. Her roommates. Old girls. Juniors. Best friends. And for B.J. McIver to look like that. Margo knew her own eyes were a nice hazelly-green and her brown hair was thick and pretty, but there was no way eyes and hair could make up for her thin face and thin, pointy nose. And even though Eva wasn't beautiful like B.J., she acted as poised and put-together as a model. Margo never looked put-together. She glanced down at herself. This morning she had put on a uniform thinking she was supposed to, then when she realized no one else was wearing one, she had meant to change but never gotten around to it. Now she felt stupid in it, especially since its golf-dress style made her look thinner than ever.

Margo hung around the front desk for a while, flipping through an old *National Geographic* and putting off the inevitable. Then she saw the young man Doug come down the stairs by himself, light a cigarette and cross the hall to the front door. Well, Margo decided, she might as well get it over with.

But the door to her room was shut and she hesitated about going in. And when she heard voices and laughter from inside, she felt like an intruder again.

24

She took a couple of deep breaths, then forced herself to knock and open the door.

But instead of stepping inside, she just stood in the doorway, staring. Her bed was stripped, her bureau drawers were open and her belongings were all over the room. Eva's mother sat in a chair smoking a cigarette. B.J. was perched on the window seat and Eva was bent over Margo's bottom bureau drawer with a pile of Margo's sweaters in her arms. At the sight of Margo, she dropped them on the bed and rushed over.

"You've got to be Margo Allinger. How absolutely marvelous!" She threw her arms around Margo and gave her a big hug. "I'm Eva Gordon, your roommate for better or worse, and over there is the infamous and notorious B.J. McIver, our suite-mate. And this is my mother, Maggie Cutler."

B.J. waved but didn't move. "Hi, welcome to the Prison on the Hill."

Mrs. Cutler stood up. She was a good-looking woman with frosted blond hair and a recent face-lift job. Margo had lived in California long enough to recognize the tight look around the eyes and the smooth, pulled expression.

"So nice to meet you, dear," Mrs. Cutler breathed in Margo's direction. Then she turned to Eva. "I must be going, Evie-dear. Doug's getting restless and I don't want him ogling all the pretty girls downstairs." She laughed a throaty, fake kind of laugh and Margo instantly didn't like her.

" 'Bye, Maggie, have fun in Spain." Eva barely looked up as her mother blew her a kiss and left.

As soon as Mrs. Cutler was gone, B.J. let out an

25

explosive howl of laughter. "My God, Eva, I can't believe Doug. How old is he anyway, twenty-five?"

"Actually he's older than he looks. He's almost thirty-two." Eva removed the last of Margo's sweaters from the drawer, opened her own suitcase and began to unpack her things into the now-empty bureau.

"So where are they going to live when they get back from Spain?" B.J. took out a pack of gum and popped two pieces in her mouth.

Eva shrugged. "Who knows? Maggie wants to stay in the New York apartment, but Doug insists on going back to Houston."

Margo didn't move. Stunned, she just stood speechless in the doorway like an actress in a play who didn't know her lines or even what the play was about. Her paralyzed state must have attracted Eva's attention. "Just so you don't get confused, Margo, which is practically impossible under the circumstances, my mother and Doug were just married and they're off tonight for a honeymoon in Spain. Doug is husband number five for Maggie-dear." Eva gave a short laugh and returned to her unpacking.

From somewhere Margo dredged up a voice, faint and feeble though it was. "But what about my bed and all my things?"

Eva smiled a wide smile and Margo saw that she had beautiful, even, white teeth. She also saw for the first time that Eva's eyes and face were perfectly made up, not too heavy, not too light, just enough to make the most of what she had. "Oh listen, Margo, I'm sorry. I should have called you or answered your cute little letter or something, but this bureau is mine and the bed next to the windows is mine, too. I had a special board put under the mattress last year for my posture. You don't mind, do you?"

"Uh . . . no, that's okay. I'm sorry. I just took the first bureau I saw." Margo blushed. It was a dumb mistake. When she saw the flowered shelf paper in all the drawers, she should have realized it was Eva's bureau.

"Hey, I'll tell you what." Eva was still smiling. "I'll be finished in a few minutes and since B.J. here lives out of a duffel bag all year long and never does unpack, we can walk into town, buy new bedspreads and curtains with the money Maggie left me, and get a decent lunch before Starch City sets in. It will be a good chance to get to know each other." Eva rushed over and impulsively gave Margo another hug, enveloping her in a cloud of fragrance. Margo stood awkwardly in her arms, not knowing what to do.

Eva pulled away first. "I can just tell by looking at you, Margo, that you're a brain," she exclaimed. "And I bet you're wonderful at things like field hockey."

"I'm not a brain at all and I've never played hockey. I play tennis."

"Of course, tennis. That's marvelous. I'm so uncoordinated I can't even connect the ball with the racket. B.J. here is big into horses while my love is the drama. The three of us complement each other perfectly, don't you think, B.J.?"

B.J. was still sitting cross-legged on the window seat. She had put on big smoked glasses but Margo

27

saw that it didn't matter. Glasses, torn sweater, dirty feet and all, she was spectacular-looking. She glanced up and saw Margo staring at her. She grinned as if she knew what Margo was thinking and it didn't impress her one way or the other.

"Sure, why not?" she answered. "The Three Musketeers, that's us."

four

Right away on the first day of classes, Margo got off to a wrong start by wearing her uniform again. As soon as she got to breakfast, she realized all the other girls were dressed in their regular clothes. How in the world did everyone know when to wear or not wear a uniform? She was so embarrassed that she bolted down her food and raced back upstairs to change. By the time she had gotten into a skirt and blouse and come back downstairs, most of the girls had already started out for classes.

Because it was raining, everyone was using the long tunnel that connected the Big Hall boarding part of the school with the rambling classroom building a couple of hundred yards away. Voices and footsteps echoed in the stone tunnel, ricocheting off the ceiling and resounding against the walls. Everyone but Margo seemed to be walking and talking with someone. Although she looked around for Eva and B.J. or any familiar face, she didn't see anyone she knew. There, up ahead, was Stretch's head above everyone else's, lurching along like a ship under sail. Cricket must have been at her side because every once in a while Stretch bent down to speak to someone Margo couldn't see. She was just about to call out to them when she overhead two girls behind her.

"Look at those weird new sophomores. I mean, they are the Mutt and Jeff of the school. And don't get in a conversation with either of them. They'll talk your ear off."

"Yeah, Cricket and Stretch. Whoever came up with those names was a genius." And the two girls laughed.

Margo slowed down and just kept on walking. She was almost at the classroom building anyway, and finding her way around would be confusing enough without getting involved with Stretch and Cricket.

Classes went better than Margo had hoped. It was a typical first day, with all the teachers giving their usual pitch about how tough the work was going to be and how the pressure would really be on. That was okay. Margo was prepared to work hard.

And then she was down to Eighth period English. Oh no, Miss Durrett *was* her English teacher, and that junior had said Miss Durrett was a terror. At least Margo was a good reader. Maybe because she had spent so much time alone, she loved to read. As she pulled out her schedule to find out where she should be, she heard her name called.

"Margo, Margo Allinger."

It was Miss Frye waving to her from down the hall. Margo waited until Miss Frye caught up to her.

"Hi, there. I was hoping I'd run into you." Miss Frye seemed glad to see her.

"Hello, Miss Frye."

"How's your first day going?"

"Fine. I think I'll like my courses. And I'm looking forward to tennis practice today."

"That's what I wanted to see you about. With this morning's rain, the courts aren't quite dry. We'll start practice at 3:45 instead of 3, then run a little later than usual."

"Okay, Miss Frye. Thanks."

"I'm glad you're coming out. See you later." Miss Frye waved and hurried off. Margo watched her go. Miss Frye wore tennis shorts and a blue shirt and brand new sneakers. The way Miss Frye walked, the way she dressed or carried herself or something, gave Margo confidence that she knew plenty about tennis. Margo could hardly wait for practice.

All of a sudden she realized she was alone in the hall. The school was ominously still with that just-before-the-buzzer silence. And then the buzzer squawked. Last period had begun and Margo didn't even know where her classroom was. She quickly checked her schedule. Room #2017. That must mean the second floor. She raced for the stairs, took them

31

three at a time, then turned left. But the numbers ran in the wrong direction. Quick, start over. But the rooms in the other direction had no numbers at all. Margo started running aimlessly as she tried to find a number, any number. Stop. Get hold of yourself. Check the map on the back of your schedule.

There it was, Room #2017 in the middle of a little dead end hall. But she didn't know where she was now in relation to where she wanted to go. The library was right behind her. Good. At least that was a starting point.

But when she got to Room #2017, the door was closed. Margo eased it open and tried to slide in, as if by not taking up much space she wouldn't be very visible. She scurried across the room to the one empty chair.

The room was totally quiet with Miss Durrett seated at her desk, looking over papers as if no one were in the room. Margo recognized her right away. She had noticed Miss Durrett last night at dinner at the next table though at the time Margo hadn't known who she was. If Miss Durrett ate in the dining room, that meant she must live on the fourth floor of Big Hall. Margo had heard someone say that the teachers who lived up there were called The Misfits. Actually, Miss Durrett didn't look like a misfit. She was pretty in a blond, colorless sort of way, with big glamour glasses that took up half her narrow face. She was in her late twenties or maybe early thirties.

There were eighteen girls in a semicircle around the room, seated in chairs with fold-down armrests. And right across the room was Cricket Goodman.

Cricket grinned and it was like seeing an old friend after a long trip.

"You're late and we have waited for you." Miss Durrett's harsh, deep voice somehow didn't match her thin paleness.

Margo blushed. It didn't take much imagination to know whom Miss Durrett was addressing. "I'm sorry . . . I . . . I got to talking to a friend . . . well, not a friend, a teacher, Miss Frye . . . and then I got lost and couldn't find this room . . ." Margo knew she was babbling like an idiot.

"Don't let it happen again. I begin and end my classes promptly." Miss Durrett slapped her notebook shut, pushed back her chair and stood up.

Margo was surprised to see how short Miss Durrett was. Seated, she had looked about Margo's height, five foot five, but standing up, she was only about five feet tall. Then she picked up two canes by the side of her desk and walked around to stand in front of the class, and Margo saw why she was so short. She was very crippled. In fact, she wore braces on both her thin, misshapen legs and large oxford orthopedic shoes.

"I'm Miss Durrett," she began, as if those were her first words to the class and nothing whatsoever had passed between Margo and her. "Now I want you new girls to get a good look at me and then forget my disability." She gave a tight little smile that never reached her eyes. "Rumor will tell you that I was in a car accident with my lover and that he was killed, leaving me not only crippled but also broken-hearted. What actually happened was a severe case of

33

childhood polio. I was desperately ill and lived in an iron lung for over a year. Consequently, I am thankful to be alive today. Now let's forget about what I look like or how I walk, and get down to the business of tenth grade English."

There was an uneasy shuffling and clearing of throats, but no one spoke or even looked at anyone else. Then, as Miss Durrett began to outline the year's work on the blackboard, the tension eased and there was the usual undercurrent of coughing and rustling papers.

The period was almost over when Miss Durrett pushed off on her canes, gave a little hop and jumped up on her desk. She sat there blinking at the class through her big glasses and Margo noticed that though she wore mascara and eye shadow, her almost lashless eyes had a curious blank expression.

"All right," she announced with a smile, "in the remaining ten minutes of the period, I would like one of you to stand up and tell us about yourself, not just your name and where you live, but what you want to get out of this year's English course and why. Are there any volunteers?"

Silence, dead silence. Margo felt her heart begin to pick up a heavy thumping rhythm, and with her peripheral vision, she could even see the pocket of her blouse rise and fall with its beat. Margo hated to talk in class. Somehow she could always get through it, but oh, not today, when she'd already gotten off to such a bad start with Miss Durrett.

"All right, if I have no volunteers, I'll take the army way and assign one." Miss Durrett reached behind her for her notebook and Margo knew she'd had it. Allinger, Margo. She was first on the rolls, always first. She wasn't even surprised when Miss Durrett called out her name, "Allinger."

Miss Durrett glanced up expectantly as a collective murmur of relief passed around the room like a sighing wind over grass. Cricket looked over at Margo with an encouraging expression on her little monkey face. A couple of the other girls looked at Margo too, then gradually as the class realized who Allinger was, everyone turned in her direction. Now Miss Durrett's attention was focused on her as well.

"So you're Allinger, are you?" The pale eyebrows arched.

"Yes." That was a dumb reply. Of course she was Allinger.

"It seems we've already heard from you today. However, perhaps you can be more enlightening this time around. Stand up, Allinger."

As Margo jumped to her feet, she brushed against her armrest and her book bag crashed to the floor in an explosion of heavy textbooks, notebooks and scattered papers. She stooped to retrieve them.

"Forget your books and begin."

Margo straightened up and looked at Miss Durrett for a cue. But Miss Durrett didn't respond in any way. She just stared at Margo, obviously waiting. Margo tried to swallow, but her mouth was so dry she couldn't even work up spit. "Uh . . . my name is Margo Allinger and I live . . . I live . . . uh . . . uh . . ." Where did she live? Not in California. Mom and Dad had sold that house. And not in New York with her sister Suzanne and brother-in-law Don. That was just her base for vacations. "Uh . . . I live here at . . . at . . ." Her mind went totally blank. She couldn't think of the name of the school. It was as if her brain had jammed and nothing was getting through. She looked over at Miss Durrett for help, but Miss Durrett's face was smoothly noncommittal. Clearly no help was coming from that direction. Then Margo heard a snicker from across the room. The sound galvanized her.

"Haywood!" Margo heard herself say loudly. She didn't know where the word came from but there it was. "The Haywood School. I live at Haywood." Her voice cracked, but at least she had unlocked the logjam of silence. Then she realized how stupid she sounded. Who lived at Haywood? No one, that's who.

Margo opened her mouth to explain, to say that her parents were overseas and that she would be spending her vacations with her sister in New York, that Haywood had to be her home and she wanted so much for it to be right, and that truly, she wasn't as dumb as she sounded. But all that came out was a faint whimper that hung a moment in the silence, then faded.

Margo looked at Miss Durrett in desperation. Help me! Her mind cried it. Her eyes pleaded it. But Miss Durrett just sat there on her desk with her misshapen legs in their braces swinging back and forth and said nothing. Her mouth was still turned up in that same half-smile.

This couldn't be happening. Margo would wake

up and the California sun would brighten her room with golden light. The smell of fresh coffee would waft upstairs and Margo would hear her father grunt and groan as he did his exercises in the next room. Then he would knock on her door and they would jog their two miles together before breakfast. Everything was all right. Margo had Dad and Dad would take care of things.

Only Margo didn't have Dad. She had only herself and it wasn't enough. She couldn't get one word out. Not one. Then they started, stupid, hateful tears welling up in her eyes and inching down her cheeks.

It was as if the tears were a signal, as if Miss Durrett had been waiting for them. "You may sit down," she snapped as she picked up her notebook and checked her list of names. "All right, Brower, suppose you give us some insight into yourself and try to stand up without disarraying your entire desk."

Margo didn't sit down so much as collapse. She was vaguely aware of the girl named Brower standing up and talking, but her mind didn't take in a word. She sensed rather than saw Cricket across the room try to catch her attention, but she couldn't raise her eyes from the floor. And then the period was over. Miss Durrett slid off her desk and, braced on her canes, addressed the class. "Read the Prologue of the *Canterbury Tales* for tomorrow and the Knight's Tale through page 40. Class dismissed."

Miss Durrett gathered up her books and limped from the room, letting the door slam behind her. There was a moment of silence before everyone was on their feet, banging down their armrests, throwing books in their book bags, scraping back their chairs. Still Margo sat there. No one spoke to her and she didn't look up as they filed from the room. It was as if she had ceased to exist. Maybe she *had* ceased to exist. She was just a nonperson, sitting at her desk surrounded by her scattered books and papers.

five

Margo quickly changed into her tennis clothes and grabbed her favorite racket. Something about the way the leather grip fit her hand was reassuring. She ran all the way down the wide staircase from her room, two steps at a time, not looking at any of the girls coming up. When she hit the bottom step, she heard someone call her name from over by the mailboxes. It was Cricket heading in her direction. Margo waved but kept going. She didn't want to see Cricket or anyone else from that English class. Not ever. Tomorrow and Miss Durrett would never come. Right now an afternoon of tennis was all there was.

A clearing wind had blown over the earlier rain, and it was a perfect September day, warm with almost no humidity. High white cotton-ball clouds punctuated a flag-blue sky. Margo enjoyed tennis most when it was warm. It kept her muscles loose and she liked the feeling of playing hard enough to work up a sweat. She ran down the long macadam driveway parallel to the tunnel connecting Big Hall with the school building. Only now, when Margo saw it from the outside, she realized it wasn't so much of a tunnel as an enclosed walkway.

As Margo zigzagged her way through the Lower School kids milling around in first day confusion looking for their buses, she was surprised to see as many boys as girls. Then she remembered that kindergarten through Eighth grade was coed and only the Upper School was all girls. For which she was grateful. If there were boys, there would be a boys' tennis team and if there were a boys' tennis team, the girls would probably never get to use the courts. Not only that, but if there were boys, it wouldn't have been just seventeen pairs of girls' eyes focused on her in English today, but boys' as well. Margo shuddered at that unpleasant image.

She skirted the Little Theater building and headed for the tennis courts at the far end of the school grounds. When she and her mother had visited Haywood last spring, the four all-weather courts were just being constructed. Now they were finished and they looked terrific. No one else had arrived yet which was what Margo had counted on. She'd come early to give herself time to look over the courts before practice began. She opened the gate to court #1 and stepped out on it. The springy still-damp green composition surface felt good underfoot. The white tape lines were brushed and clean. Margo was on home territory. Most schools had macadam courts with ripped nets, painted lines and weeds poking through the cracks. These were the best school courts she had ever seen.

"Hi there."

Margo hadn't even heard the sound of a motor, but a jeep had pulled up onto the grass and parked. Miss Frye stuck out her head and waved.

"Hi." Margo waved too.

Miss Frye grinned as she climbed out of the jeep. She had a deep dimple in one cheek but not in the other, which gave her a lopsided, gamin look that made it impossible not to smile back. As Miss Frye walked around to the back of her jeep to unload her equipment, Margo ran over to help her.

"This is a real first," Miss Frye said as she handed Margo a huge net bag of practice balls. "I can't ever remember anyone getting to practice before me or helping me set up. Thanks, Allie."

Allie. Margo felt herself blush. She had always wanted a nickname, but this was the first time she could ever remember being called anything but Margo, except for one dreadful sixth grade year when all the kids had called her Mouse.

Margo held the gate open for Miss Frye and followed her out onto the courts.

"These courts are great, Miss Frye," Margo said.

"Well, let me tell you, getting them was a real hassle. I had to fight like mad for the money, but now that they're done everyone is pleased, especially me. Our tennis program is the best in the area and I intend to keep it that way."

What a beautiful voice Miss Frye had, rather high, but soft and musical. Margo set the bag of practice balls by the fence as Miss Frye began to limber up.

"I think the courts are dry enough to play on. How about hitting a few balls while we wait for the rest of the team?" Miss Frye picked up her racket.

"Sure." Margo did a couple of knee bends and twists to loosen up as Miss Frye took the far side of the court.

They started out slowly, just hitting easy at first, not even going all the way back to the baseline. Then Miss Frye began to pick up the tempo, a little harder, a little deeper, a little more spin on the ball. And Margo did the same. It was astounding. Their games really matched. Miss Frye was far better than Margo, but their styles were surprisingly similar. They built up a kind of rhythm that was exciting, and Margo could tell by the concentrated way Miss Frye was hitting the ball that she too sensed how well their games meshed. As Margo rallied, the whole miserable day fell away from her as if it had never happened. All she was aware of was the solid thunk of the ball on her strings and her body moving the way she wanted it to.

"How about trying some at net?" Miss Frye called. Playing net was the weakest part of Margo's game, but today even that went better. It was as if Miss Frye brought out the very best in her.

42

"That's enough for now, Allie." Miss Frye joined Margo at net. "You need help on your net game, but otherwise your strokes look good, especially your backhand. Now let's put some of those lazies over there to work." Miss Frye gestured toward the fence.

Surprised, Margo turned around. With her back to the driveway, she hadn't noticed that the rest of the team had arrived. They were seated on the grass watching her and Miss Frye, and right away Margo realized she was in the wrong clothes again. She had worn a tennis dress and everyone else was in cut-offs or a gym suit. Maybe that was why they were all staring at her. Or maybe it was because they had heard about what had happened to her in English class. But that was ridiculous. English class was just last period. There was no way they could have heard.

"Hi, gang," Miss Frye sang out. "Welcome to Frye's Work Camp for Backward and Delinquent Females."

A couple of the girls laughed. Then a big red-headed girl stood up and stepped forward. She was tall and heavy, almost fat, and she looked older than the others, at least eighteen. And she wasn't laughing.

Miss Frye's hand came down on Margo's shoulder. "Allie, this is Trish Kinkead. Trish, Allie Allinger. Trish is our captain and number one player, Allie. She's ranked second in the whole Philadelphia area. I'd like you to hit some with Allie if you would, Trish. She has a whole lot of potential. I even see her as a possibility for third singles."

The expression on Trish's pale freckled face hadn't been noticeably friendly, but now it looked as shocked as if she had just witnessed an accident. Everyone else froze, too. There was such a complete silence Margo was aware of the traffic swishing by on the street beyond the high hedges bordering the school grounds.

Apparently Miss Frye didn't notice the tension. She began to call out names and assignments as the girls got to their feet and straggled out onto the courts. "Okay, Allie and Trish play singles, Phoebe and Izzy are another singles, and the rest of you scramble it up any way you want in doubles."

Now everyone had gone out on the courts except Trish and Margo. Trish just stood there looking at Margo from a good five inch advantage. Her eyes were dark, dark brown and there was no way, from looking at them, that Margo could tell what she was thinking. Then Trish opened the gate and led the way out onto the first court. "Okay, Allie, let's see what you can do."

There was no mistaking the inflection in her voice. The 'Allie' was loaded with sarcasm.

Trish was a senior and captain of the team. The last thing Margo wanted right now was to alienate Trish before the season had even begun. "Actually my name is Margo Allinger," she offered in the pleasantest way she knew.

"Okay, then Margo Allinger it is. I wouldn't dream of intruding on a private nickname." This time Trish smiled, but her smile was about as friendly as an opponent's at match point.

six

It wasn't until Margo and Eva were back in their room after supper that Eva mentioned what had happened in English. Margo was hoping Eva hadn't heard about it. She was, in fact, hoping that no one had heard about it. In the back of her mind, she was hoping it had never happened. But right away, Eva brought up the subject.

"I hear that Durrett really socked it to you today."

She mentioned it so casually Margo wasn't even sure she had said it. Eva's stereo was on high, and she was all concentration plucking her eyebrows in front of one of those makeup mirrors surrounded by little

45

white lights. The words in Margo's social studies book jiggled and ran together.

"What?"

"I said I hear that Durrett really gave it to you in class today."

This time there was no mistaking what she said. "Uh . . . yeah, I guess she did."

B.J. couldn't possibly have heard their conversation from her room over the blare of the stereo, but all of a sudden there she was, standing in the doorway to the bathroom that separated the two bedrooms. She didn't say anything. She just leaned against the doorjamb, smelling faintly of horse and chewing bubble gum.

Eva kept on plucking her eyebrows. "Durrett's just a sawed-off cripple who's jealous because you're such a terrific jock. Still, a certified bitch like that will probe to find a weak point, then wham, let you have it. The trick is, you've got to prove that you're the one in control and not her. I learned that the hard way when I was eleven and realized the stepfather I was so crazy about was just using me to get to my mother and didn't care about me at all. Believe me, since then I've never let anyone push me around. Control's the name of the game and Durrett's a master."

Eva was right. Margo had felt like a puppet on Miss Durrett's strings today. Even now she could see Miss Durrett's triumphant pale eyes behind those huge glasses. Still, it was easy for Eva to stay in control. She had lots of self-confidence. Nothing fazed her. Not like Margo. No matter how badly Margo wanted to do the right thing, she always seemed to do everything wrong.

B.J. threw in her two cents. "Your whole problem is that you're too uptight, Margo. You gotta stay loose and laid back, you know, like me." As if to prove her point, B.J. blew an enormous blue bubble.

That was no news to Margo. She knew she was too serious. She was just going to have to force herself to loosen up. "Well, you have to realize with an IQ of 65, it's hard to remember my own name, let alone where I live." It wasn't much, but it was the best she could do.

Surprisingly, B.J. chuckled and Eva laughed too. Then Eva turned from her mirror and looked at Margo directly. "Listen, Margo, it's like B.J. said before, we're the Three Musketeers and no matter what, B.J. and I will stick up for you. That's what friends are for. And we're always around to help you. It's freaks like those new girls, Crickie-Pooh and Stretch, or whatever their silly names are, who don't know how to handle themselves. They obviously don't even care that everyone thinks they're ridiculous. B.J. and I would never let that happen to you."

Cricket and Stretch *didn't* seem to care what people thought of them. All of a sudden, Margo felt sorry for them. Here they were, among the few new sophomores in the school just like she was, but they had no one to stand behind them the way she had Eva and B.J. It was funny. Margo had been worried about being the new girl with two old girls and actually it couldn't have worked out better.

The next morning Margo went down to the dining room alone as usual. Eva and B.J. never ate breakfast. Eva was on a diet and B.J. always slept until the last possible moment. Only two sign-outs a week were allowed for missing breakfast, so Eva had asked Margo to sign B.J.'s and her initials on the register slips for the other five days. Margo didn't mind helping out. She never missed breakfast. It was her favorite meal of the day. As she walked down the stairs anticipating the eggs and sausages she could smell cooking, she heard Stretch call her name. She hesitated. She just bet Stretch and Cricket wanted to eat with her. Margo remembered what Eva had said about them the night before and she wished they hadn't seen her. Still, there was no getting out of it now. They had already caught up to her.

Trying not to be obvious, Margo led the way over to a dark corner table, hoping no one would notice them. But four girls in yellow senior blazers who had been standing by the door, followed them right over and sat down. With a start, Margo realized that one of them was Trish and two of them were on the tennis team although she didn't remember their names. Trish wore a little gold tennis racket on her blazer with 'Captain' engraved on it.

"Hi, Allinger." Trish seemed friendly enough.

"Hi, Trish." Margo was determined to be pleasant although Trish had hardly spoken a word the whole time they had played yesterday. Margo gestured toward Cricket and Stretch. "This is Cricket Goodman and . . . and . . ." Stretch Strennett sounded silly. ". . . this is Jill Strennett. This is Trish," she finished lamely, not remembering Trish's last name.

"Trish Kinkead," Trish supplied. "And this is Ginger Ott my roommate, and you know my other roommates Izzy Coward and Phoebe Richmond from

48

the tennis team. This is Margo Allinger, Haywood's newest tennis wonder."

Margo didn't allow herself to hear the cutting edge to Trish's voice. She just said hello all around and started eating. The food was good, hot scrambled eggs and sausages. She spread a thick layer of marmalade on her toast. She could eat and eat and never gain weight. In fact she wished she could gain weight. The rest of the table was quiet, too, as everyone settled down to eating. Then unexpectedly, Cricket leaned around Stretch and spoke to Margo.

"What class do you have Seventh period, Margo?"

Why would she want to know that? "Math."

"I'm at that end of the building Seventh period, too. Why don't I meet you in front of Study Hall and we'll go to English together."

As if on signal, every head at the table snapped up and every face expressed curiosity. As for Margo, she just kept on eating, shoveling down the scrambled eggs as if she couldn't get enough.

"Okay, fine," she mumbled, wishing Cricket would keep quiet.

For a few minutes, the only sound at the table was the clink of silver and the surrounding high-pitched hum of a hundred female voices. Then Trish put down her fork and looked right at Margo. "Thank God I have Mrs. Jordan for senior English instead of Durrett," she said casually. "Durrett gives rotten grades to seniors just to make sure their records for college look bad."

Margo didn't raise her head but she felt every eye on her.

"I had Durrett sophomore year and almost failed."

Phoebe's tone was as casual as Trish's. Phoebe was a short, muscular, brown haired girl with brown eyes and a dark tan so that she seemed the same color all over. Now her wide eyes were all innocence as she looked at Margo. "You have Durrett for sophomore English, don't you?"

At that moment, Margo knew that these four seniors had somehow heard about what had happened to her in Miss Durrett's class. How had word gotten around so fast? All of a sudden she wondered if the whole school knew. Maybe they were all talking about her right now. The sophomore who couldn't get two words out, who didn't know where she lived or what school she went to. Although her stomach was a great hard lump, she couldn't raise her head from her plate or stop eating.

"It's a funny thing about Durrett," Phoebe continued as if she hadn't expected Margo to answer, "but she likes to zero in on one person and . . ."

"Let me tell you, I am mighty glad I don't have Durrett," Stretch interrupted in a loud voice that cut Phoebe right off. "English is my worst subject and I'll be lucky to get through it. Now Biology is something else again. Mr. Hopkins is going to be the greatest, I just know it. Yesterday he told us we'll be dissecting rats next week. I can't wait to . . ."

Stretch looked around the table as if she just assumed everyone was terribly interested in dissecting rats. As she kept up her monologue, the four seniors exchanged disgusted looks. Then at a nod from Trish, they all stood up and left the table. Still Stretch kept on talking. She didn't let up until the seniors were out of the dining room.

50

Then she blew all the air out of her lungs. "Whew, how's that for shutting up those Barbie dolls? I considered describing the dissection of a dead racoon I found last summer, but decided that might turn even my stomach." Stretch's wide mouth broke into a grin.

Cricket laughed and shook her head. "Stretch, you are too much. Who would come up with rats but you?"

Margo knew that Stretch had saved her from a really embarrassing situation. She should have been grateful. She wanted to be grateful. But Stretch had put her on the spot. Those seniors had been really annoyed, and whether Stretch knew it or not, they were furious at her. Not only that, but now they associated Margo with Stretch and Cricket, and at this point, that was an association she could very well do without.

seven

That afternoon, like it or not, Cricket met Margo after Math and they went to English together. Although they made it before the period began, they were the last to arrive and Margo couldn't look at one single face as she hurried across the room to her chair. Miss Durrett was already seated on her desk which apparently was her favorite perch, maybe because it made her seem taller than anyone else.

As it turned out, Miss Durrett couldn't have been more entertaining. The class was starting Chaucer, and though some of the lines and phrases had gone over Margo's head when she read it, Miss Durrett made it all come together. She didn't call on anyone

52

the whole period and never even looked at Margo. Still, when Margo got up from her chair at the end of class, she was as stiff and sore as if she had been lifting weights.

Although Margo anticipated the worst all week, classes went okay and Miss Durrett didn't call on her once. Tennis was going both well and not well. As the days went by, Margo was finally able to put team names and faces together, and to her great delight, Miss Frye had decided to play her at third singles. Trish would play first singles, Izzy Coward second singles and Margo third. But despite the fact that Margo pushed herself to be friendly, everyone on the team practically ignored her. Before and after practice when the girls gathered in groups to talk and hack around, Margo was never included, and if anyone ever did speak to her, they called her Allinger the way Trish did. Bewildered and hurt, Margo couldn't figure it out. These were the girls she had counted on to be her friends.

At least Miss Frye had been terrific about helping her with her game. Maybe it was because Margo was the only sophomore on the varsity that Miss Frye was giving her extra help. Twice she had worked out a full hour with Margo after team practice, and on Friday, she asked if Margo would like to play tennis with her on Saturday at a little local club she belonged to and have lunch afterwards.

The invitation came at a perfect time. Eva and B.J. were spending Saturday with two boys from Lewiston Academy. Scott Peterson and Gavin Rhodes were all Margo had heard about for days. Though Eva and B.J. said they couldn't wait for Margo to meet their boy friends, she very well could. Scott and Gavin were seniors, big lacrosse stars and both were applying to Princeton. Margo was sure they were handsome, witty and smooth, all the qualities guaranteed to tie her up in knots. Now that she was spending Saturday with Miss Frye, she didn't even have to think up an excuse not to meet them.

Margo's sneakers hardly made any noise as she raced across Big Hall Saturday morning. Miss Frye was due to pick her up by the front porch at 11:30, but Margo decided to wait out by the entrance gates to save time. She was early. She leaned against the huge stone pillar with its discreet brass plaque, *The Haywood School, Established 1902. Studies Pass into Character,* and looked back at Big Hall. With its huge round tower, curved front porch, stone facade and rows of endless windows, it was a strange architectural combination of handsome and hideous. It had probably been a super-fashionable hotel a hundred years ago and Margo could picture its genteel Philadelphia guests rocking on the long side porch or driving in carriages up the curving front drive with its border of beautiful cherry trees.

Margo's great-aunt had graduated from Haywood a million years ago, and then gone on to Wellesley. College. Margo hadn't even thought about college. Her sister Suzanne had gone only for a year, and then married Don. She must have been crazy. Marriage seemed even more remote than college. Living with one person forever and ever. Margo couldn't imagine it.

Honk-a-honk.

It was the jeep's harsh horn. Miss Frye had pulled up without Margo noticing. She leaned out the window. "Hop in, Allie. Just throw your things in the back."

Miss Frye was dressed for tennis, too, in white shorts and white shirt with a blue band around her short blond hair. No matter what Miss Frye had on, she always wore something pale blue that picked up the color of her eyes. And she was smiling. Maybe it was her smile that made her glow with health or fun or humor or something. Or maybe it was her tan that made her glow. Whatever it was, Margo enjoyed being with her. She relaxed against the seat and watched Miss Frye's small, competent hands maneuver the jeep through heavy Saturday traffic.

"Unless you're absolutely famished, we can play for a couple of hours and then go back to my place for lunch, Allie."

"That sounds fine."

"Women can't play at our little Greenbrook Club until noon. It's infuriating, but so far I've had no luck trying to get the rules changed. Someday the Board members will have to acknowledge the fact they're living in the twentieth century." Miss Frye laughed, but she didn't sound as if she thought it was very funny.

Greenbrook Club really was little. Three courts were plunked down in the middle of a residential neighborhood with just a gazebo-kind of overhang for a clubhouse. The place was low-key like Miss Frye, and right away Margo liked it. Men were milling around, talking, drinking cokes and gathering up

55

their things to leave. Everyone seemed to know everyone else and when Miss Frye introduced Margo around, all the men were friendly. Two sets of doubles were using the far courts, while two boys were playing singles on the first court.

Miss Frye cupped her hands and shouted out to them. "Hey, Pete, haven't you been playing long enough? How about giving some decent players a chance?"

The younger of the two boys, the one who must have been Pete, looked over and waved. "We're almost done."

Margo watched as they finished. Pete looked high school age, maybe sixteen or seventeen. He was short, about Margo's height, and really skinny, with wild red hair that stuck out in every direction and funny bowed legs. He had basically good form, but he drove the ball all over the place, hitting it out or smashing it into the net. His opponent looked four or five years older. He was taller, more muscular, better-looking and a better player. He ended the match with an unreachable lob over Pete's head.

When they came off the court, Miss Frye introduced Margo. "Pete and Johnny Montgomery, Allie. This is one of my new students, boys, a sophomore, Allie Allinger."

Now why did Miss Frye have to go and announce that she was a sophomore? It made her sound about ten years old. But Margo felt better when both boys, who must be brothers, she realized, although they looked nothing alike, shook hands with her, first Johnny, the older one, then Pete, the redhead. It was the first time anyone her age had done that and she liked it.

"So you go to Haywood, do you, Allie?" Johnny asked.

Margo nodded. "I just started this fall."

Johnny winked. "Watch out for those Wycliffe High School boys, Allie. They're a dangerous bunch and I ought to know. I used to be one. And Pete here is the worst of the lot." He leaned over and punched Pete on the arm.

"Actually I'm a veddy nice fellow . . ." Pete began in a phony kind of accent.

But Miss Frye didn't let him finish. "Come on, Allie, let's get going." She jumped up from the bench and headed for the gate. Since no one else was waiting to play, Margo didn't see what the hurry was, but she followed Miss Frye out onto the court. As they got ready to start, Johnny picked up his racket and sweater and left, although Margo noticed that Pete got himself a coke and settled down on the bench to watch.

Miss Frye must have felt at home on her own courts. She had always been thoughtful before about holding back and not putting the ball away on every shot the way Margo knew she could. But now she seemed determined to show what she could do and she just about blasted Margo off the court. Even in the warm-up, she forced Margo to come to net, then put the ball down the sideline out of reach or lobbed it high over Margo's head. And she looked serious, too, as if she meant business.

By the time they started playing, Margo was already hot and panting. And she didn't win a single point in the first two games. Not one. She was scrambling and charging around the court like a beginner as she tried to return Miss Frye's impossible shots.

"So long, Allie. I'll see you around. Goodbye, Miss Frye." It was Pete. He was standing up, ready to leave.

Margo waved. "So long, Pete." She knew her face was red with exertion and her shirttails were out. More than that, she was embarrassed that Pete had seen her play so badly. She couldn't ever remember looking worse.

Margo got a couple of points in the next game, but it wasn't until the fourth game that she realized she was doing better. Not that Miss Frye wasn't still winning, but Margo's game seemed smoother and less frantic. Then she realized it wasn't she who was better, it was Miss Frye who was making her look better. Margo's game depended on Miss Frye's game. Well, who did Margo think she was anyway? She was lucky Miss Frye was even willing to play with her. They played for another hour and a half and ended up having a great time. And Miss Frye was her old self again, smiling and kidding around and even letting Margo win an occasional game.

Miss Frye's apartment wasn't far from the club. It was the rambling third floor of a big old Victorian house. The long, narrow living room, painted white, was light and airy and the big bay windows were a burst of green and flowering plants. The furniture was a mixture of modern and antique with lots of comfortable-looking stuffed chairs.

"Why don't you shower and change, Allie, while I get lunch?" Miss Frye showed Margo into a big, high-ceilinged bathroom with old-fashioned fixtures. By the time Margo was finished and dressed, Miss Frye had set up lunch in the bay window—cold soup, shrimp salad and tall glasses of iced tea. It looked delicious.

While Margo waited for Miss Frye to shower and change, she studied the view out the bay windows. It was a neighborhood of big old houses like this one, probably all divided up into apartments, too. Margo wondered how long Miss Frye had lived here . . . where she was from . . . how many years she had been at Haywood . . . if she'd ever been married. Somehow Margo couldn't picture Miss Frye with a husband. Marriage was too ordinary for Miss Frye. She was too alive to be tied down to one person. She was just about the most alive person Margo had ever known.

Miss Frye wasn't gone long and when she appeared, she surprised Margo by looking somehow different. She wore a long-sleeved white blouse and white slacks with a blue scarf around her neck. It was the first time Margo had seen her in anything but tennis clothes or a gym uniform. This outfit made her look prettier, softer, something Margo couldn't put her finger on.

"How could you resist starting, Allie? I'm starved."

Margo glanced up and smiled. "It looks delicious, Miss Frye. I love shrimp."

Miss Frye sat down and took a sip of her iced tea. "All this Miss Frye business is rather silly, isn't it?

One of the rules of our little Greenbrook Club is that everyone is on a first name basis and since we'll be doing this again, you might as well call me Virginia, at least away from school, don't you think?"

Margo hesitated. She remembered that neither Johnny nor Pete Montgomery had called her Virginia. Besides, a teacher was a teacher, even a terrific one like Miss Frye. Somehow Margo couldn't imagine herself ever calling Miss Frye Virginia. She ducked her head and took a long swallow of iced tea so she wouldn't have to answer.

eight

The next couple of weeks went okay. The school work was hard, and though Margo wasn't doing great, at least she was passing everything. She and Eva and B.J. had a few ups and downs, but basically they got along well. Every Wednesday night they skipped dinner, went into town and pigged out on junk food, all Eva's treat, though Margo noticed Eva didn't eat anywhere near as much as she and B.J. did. And Eva and B.J. showed her how to get into the Big Hall recreation room after hours to watch the late, late movie on TV. The only thing Margo wasn't crazy about was covering up for Eva and B.J. the way

61

they wanted her to when they got in past the night curfew hour, smelling of beer and acting silly.

Unfortunately, the tennis team continued to be a problem. No matter what Margo did to be friendly, her teammates would hardly give her the time of day, especially the seniors. They rallied and practiced with her, but only under Miss Frye's direction. Otherwise they left her alone and no one ever asked her to hit some or even fill in for a pickup game. They acted as if Margo didn't exist. She couldn't understand it. She knew it wasn't her game because her game had never been better. She and Miss Frye played at Greenbrook Club every Saturday and the extra practice was improving her strokes tremendously. Whatever the reason, the way the team treated her kept Margo on edge.

Then it was Friday of Margo's biggest weekend yet. After tennis practice, she was leaving to visit her sister and brother-in-law in New York. Anticipation of the weekend ahead, combined with a warm, hazy October afternoon, had Margo lazily daydreaming as Miss Durrett droned on in Eighth period English. The sun streamed through the windows, warming Margo into a kind of stupor. She hadn't heard a word of the lecture.

"Stand up, Allinger, and give us your thoughts on the subject."

It was Miss Durrett's grating voice, as strident as a chain saw. Margo jerked her head up. She wasn't even certain it was her name that had been called until she saw Miss Durrett's self-satisfied little smile directed at her.

"Well, Allinger?"

"Stand up," someone nearby hissed.

Margo didn't know where the voice had come from, but in a reflex action, she jumped to her feet.

"Well, that's the first step, Allinger." Miss Durrett chuckled and a few of the girls laughed, too. "Now let's hear your ideas."

Ideas about what? Chaucer, they were still studying Chaucer, Margo knew that, but she hadn't a clue as to what Miss Durrett wanted of her. "Well . . . I'd have to say . . . that . . . uh . . ."

That was when it happened. Margo's throat closed up just as it had that first day. It was like someone had their hands around her throat choking off her air. She felt lightheaded from the pressure.

"Sst . . . sst . . . The Wife of Bath . . . sst . . ."

It was the same whispery voice prompting her. Something about the Wife of Bath. But what about the Wife of Bath? Margo's mind was blank. She tried to swallow but couldn't get anything past the ring of iron that bound her throat. For some stupid reason, she thought of those black water birds in China that wore rings around their necks so they couldn't swallow the fish they caught for their masters. That was exactly how she felt.

"Well-ll?" Miss Durrett stretched the word out.

Now the room was tensely silent. The faces looking up at Margo were pale blurs. Then from somewhere within her, words began to blurt out. "Well . . . uh . . . the Wife of Bath was a widow . . . she was . . . uh . . . married five times and uh . . . uh . . ." The end. That was all there was. Margo waited for more as if it would come of its own volition, but nothing happened.

"Sst . . . sst . . . sst . . ." came that whisper again. But Margo couldn't make out the words. It was as if her hearing were as blocked as her speech. Or maybe it was the ringing in her ears that drowned out the sound.

"Goodman, if you're so anxious to talk I'll give you plenty of opportunity later, but since we haven't heard from Allinger in some time, we'll wait to hear what she has to say." And Miss Durrett gave that humorless little chuckle again.

The same nervous giggle travelled around the room as it vaguely registered on Margo that it was Cricket Goodman trying to help her. It was too late. The circuits in her brain were scrambled. "I . . . I don't know the answer . . ." Just the effort of getting out those few words was an exertion, and her knees went so weak that she had to brace herself against her desk.

"Now you don't strike me as stupid, Allinger. In fact, you strike me as reasonably intelligent." Miss Durrett sounded as matter-of-fact as if she were discussing the weather. "And by the results of yesterday's quiz, I'd say you know at least something about the Wife of Bath. So please share your opinions with us."

Miss Durrett was smiling so that her small, even, white teeth showed. Then her pointed pink tongue darted in and out like a serpent's. She was like that snake in India that mesmerized its prey so the creature couldn't cry out or make any kind of escape. Then, when the snake was ready, it moved in for the kill. Margo was that victim, incapable of uttering a sound or moving to defend herself. Abruptly, she sat down. Her teeth were clenched so tight her jaws ached.

"But I didn't say you could sit down yet, Allinger. Sitting down on your own accord will give you an automatic zero."

Margo bit her lip and shook her head. She couldn't stand up again no matter what.

Miss Durrett arranged her face in a worried expression. "What a shame, Allinger. That means a zero and as you know, a zero won't help your average one bit." She made a notation in her notebook, then turned to Cricket. "All right, Goodman, if you're so anxious to talk let's hear what you have to say."

There was a brief moment when Cricket stared up at Miss Durrett, still seated on her desk. The whole class was so quiet that the sound of a fly dive-bombing against the window filled the room. For a second, for a brief second, Margo quickened with the hope that Cricket wasn't going to stand up and answer. She *prayed* that Cricket wouldn't stand up and answer. It was too much to hope for. Cricket's chair screeched along the floor as she got to her feet.

Rat-a-tat, rat-a-tat, rat-a-tat. Margo couldn't make out one coherent word Cricket said as waves of nausea washed over her. It took all her concentration not to be sick. And her hands were icy cold in her lap.

At last, at long last, the buzzer sounded. This time Margo was the first out of the room. She grabbed her books, threw them in her book bag and ran out the door even before Miss Durrett assigned the homework. She raced the length of the empty hall, clattered down the stairs in her noisy clogs, pushed open the heavy fire exit door and rushed outside. The trees were a burst of dazzling October color as she flew up the driveway toward Big Hall.

"Margo, wait for me!" That was Cricket yelling at her. Cricket must have run from the room too. But Margo didn't turn around. She didn't want to see Cricket. She didn't want to see anyone. All she wanted now was to reach her room, pack, and get out of here.

Margo pushed her way through the lines of Lower School kids waiting for their buses. What had happened to her? She had never liked talking in class, but she had always been able to do it. Now she couldn't get a word out. It was as if Miss Durrett had put her under some terrible spell. Miss Durrett was a witch, that's what she was. Even now Margo could see her smirking face with those little white teeth. She was a monstrous, evil smile, disembodied from her thin, long-waisted body and distorted legs. Margo ran up the front porch steps and into Big Hall.

"Aren't you coming to practice, Margo?"

It was Cathy, one of the sophomore substitutes on the tennis team coming down the front stairs in her gym suit and sneakers as Margo went up. Margo brushed right past her without answering. No! No! No! She wasn't going anywhere but New York. She had to see Suzanne and Don. She had to talk to them, beg them to let her stay with them and go to school in New York until Mom and Dad came home. When Margo came down these stairs again, it would be for the last time. She was never coming back to Haywood. Not ever.

nine

Margo had never seen a sight so wonderful as Suzanne and Don when she arrived at their apartment that evening. They lived in the East Fifties and she didn't wait for a bus or even try to find the right subway. She just took a taxi right up from the station.

"Oh, Suzanne, it's so good to see you." Margo burst out crying as she threw her arms first around Suzanne, then around Don.

Suzanne returned her hug with a sympathetic laugh, then held her at arm's length. "Margo, honey, what's wrong?"

"Suzanne, I can't go back to Haywood. I just can't

... there's this awful teacher ... and no one on the tennis team likes me ... and ... and can I move in with you two? Just until Mom and Dad get back. I won't be in the way and I can go to public high school right here in New York and save Dad a lot of money. He could even pay you for my room and board."

Upset as she was, Margo couldn't help noticing Suzanne and Don exchange worried glances. "Well, honey, that's not so easy. You see ..." Suzanne began.

Don didn't let her finish. "Margo, you haven't even taken off your coat or put your bag down." Don's laugh was overly cheerful as he took Margo's overnight case from her hand. "We haven't seen you for months and we have lots of catching up to do."

Margo followed Suzanne and Don into their tiny living room with the ominous feeling that things weren't going the way she had planned. Suzanne had the stereo on playing her usual musical show tapes, and as soon as they sat down, she started talking about what she'd heard from Mom and Dad and about her job and about Don's new job. Then she told Margo the big news. She was pregnant. Margo looked at her, really looked at her, for the first time. Even though Suzanne wore a loose-fitting blouse, Margo could see she had gained weight. No, Margo wouldn't tell Mom and Dad yet. Yes, the news was terrific and she was really happy for them.

They were all wound up in their own plans. Suzanne was going to work until after Christmas and then spend her last six weeks fixing up the little guest room into a nursery. Suzanne and Don were going to maternity classes. Don planned to help at the delivery. Suzanne wanted to nurse the baby. Margo tried to act interested, but through all her congratulations and enthusiasm, the hard lump of knowledge lay like a weight in her chest that this new baby was cancelling her right out of Suzanne and Don's life.

Suzanne must have sensed what Margo was thinking. She jumped up from her chair, ran over and took both of Margo's hands in hers. "Honey, this baby won't make any difference at all as far as you're concerned. When you come to visit, the baby can sleep right here in the living room."

Visit. That was the word Suzanne used. But Margo didn't want to visit. She wanted to live here. It wasn't possible. In her gentle, tactful way Suzanne was telling her there wasn't room. And Margo got the message loud and clear. So none of them mentioned Margo moving in with them again. It was as if they were all pretending she had never asked. As they sat talking about the baby, Margo began to sort through other possibilities. There weren't many. Though Dad's parents were alive and well, they lived in a retirement community out in Seattle. Mom had a sister, but she was divorced and working as some big executive in a Kansas City department store. She'd want Margo around like a hole in the head.

So that was that. Margo was stuck with Haywood. But tonight was Friday night and she had two whole days with Suzanne and Don before she had to go back. She refused to let herself even think about Haywood. Swoosh, she mentally swept it right out of her head.

69

Surprisingly enough, it worked. She slept almost until noon on Saturday, and Suzanne and Don kept her on the go until after midnight, when they had a late dinner at Luchow's after an Off-Broadway show. Even church on Sunday wasn't bad. Margo couldn't help but think how settled and square Suzanne and Don were. She couldn't imagine their life style for herself, not even in ten years. Yet there was something comfortable about it, too. Neither Suzanne nor Don ever seemed to struggle and agonize over everything the way she did, torn first one way, then another.

Margo did her best all weekend to be as cheerful and pleasant as Suzanne and Don were. She limited herself to talking about how she and Eva and B.J. were great pals and did everything together. And she told them about Miss Frye and how terrific she was and how they played tennis every Saturday and went to her apartment afterwards for lunch, and how she had even asked Margo to call her Virginia which Margo hadn't been able to do yet.

Then it was Sunday afternoon. Margo had just started packing when Suzanne knocked on her door and came in. She helped Margo fold up the hide-a-bed, then sat down on it, patting the seat next to her for Margo to sit down, too. She put one hand around Margo's shoulders and with the other brushed back Margo's bangs.

"I'd love to see you let your hair grow, Margo. Wearing it short with bangs was fine when you were little, but you're growing up now. And if your hair were back from your forehead, it would set off your

70

beautiful eyes. I always wished I had eyes like yours instead of being stuck with eyes just like Dad's." Suzanne squinted up her eyes and made a ridiculous face.

Margo laughed. "That's silly, Suzanne. You're the one who's beautiful, not me."

They sat for a moment without speaking, then Suzanne got up and walked to the window. Her expression was serious and Margo realized that Suzanne must have had some reason for coming in. She did.

"When you arrived, Margo," Suzanne began, "you mentioned that the tennis team didn't like you and you had some terrible teacher. You seemed awfully upset. Do you want to talk about it?"

Margo didn't say anything for a minute. She was tempted to pour it all out and tell Suzanne how Miss Durrett had humiliated her. Devastated her. But that wouldn't accomplish anything. Suzanne couldn't help from a distance, and since there was no way Margo could leave Haywood anyhow, what was the point of hashing it all over? As for the tennis team, Suzanne couldn't do anything to help there either. Margo herself didn't know what was wrong. No, telling Suzanne her problems would just make them worse. For now, it was better to keep everything cheerful and pleasant the way it had been all weekend.

"Oh, you know, Suzanne, it's always been hard for me to make friends and everyone on the tennis team knows each other already. It'll work out. As for my English teacher, it's just that we don't get along. Nobody can stand her and I got stuck with her this year. That's all."

"I'm sorry, Margo, but I guess we all meet up with

a lemon at some point in school. I know I did. Mrs. Graver in Eighth grade. What a pill she was." Suzanne smiled sympathetically. If she suspected Margo was worried about anything more serious, she didn't let on. She came back to the sofa and sat down again.

"Since we're on the subject of Haywood, Margo, Don and I were talking just this morning about your being at an all-girls' school. You do get a chance to meet boys, don't you, at mixers or dances or some place? I mean, Miss Frye and tennis sound perfectly fine, but it seems to me it would be more fun to spend weekends with people your own age."

"My weekends are fine. I have a good time." Margo wasn't about to let Suzanne put down the one thing that kept her going at Haywood. Miss Frye was much too important to her. And for some reason, Suzanne was making her feel guilty. Margo jumped up and started packing busily. At least Suzanne had the good sense to realize Margo didn't want to talk about it any more. She got up, too, and went to fix an early supper.

It was a relief to have Suzanne go. Right now, just the mention of Haywood had knotted up her stomach and Margo didn't need any more pressure. She had sworn she would never go back yet here she was, ready to return. For the moment, that sobering fact was as much as she could handle.

ten

By coincidence, the first people Margo saw when she got back to Haywood that night were Eva and B.J. They were on the front porch saying good night to their boy friends. They were half-hidden in the shadows of the porch overhang, two sets of merged figures. Margo stopped at the foot of the stairs. She didn't know whether to speak or pretend she hadn't seen them. She decided just to keep on going.

But Eva spotted her. "Margo, is that you?" she called out.

Now Margo had no choice but to stop as both pairs separated and moved apart. Eva strolled over into the circle of yellow porch light and signaled for her boy friend to follow. B.J. didn't move. She just slumped against the wall and lit a cigarette, though smoking wasn't allowed out here.

Eva didn't seem the least bit flustered. "Margo, this is Scott Peterson. Scott, this is Margo Allinger, the roommate I've told you so much about. You know, the one who's such a terrific tennis player. Weren't B.J. and I lucky to get such a great roommate sight unseen?"

Margo certainly didn't feel great. She felt stupid as she stood there clutching her overnight case as if someone were about to steal it.

"Hi, Scott," she said. Remembering how impressed she had been with Pete and Johnny Montgomery shaking hands with her, she put out her hand. Apparently her gesture caught Scott offguard. He hesitated. Then, as Margo pulled her hand back, he stuck his out and they ended up in an awkward, mismatched handshake.

Eva slipped her arm through Scott's and looked up at him. "Don't you think Margo and Roger would hit it off, Scott? You've heard me talk about Roger Munson, Margo. He's Scott's roommate and a terrific guy."

If he were anything like Scott, Margo guessed he probably was. Scott was tall, blond and good-looking. His piercing dark eyes practically glowed in the dark. But he was noticeably unenthusiastic. "I don't know, Eva. Roger's got some new babe back home."

"So what? She's not around and Margo is. Right, Margo?"

Luckily, B.J. saved Margo from having to reply.

74

She had meandered over hand in hand with the boy Margo assumed was Gavin, although B.J. never introduced him.

"How was your weekend in New York?" B.J. asked, tossing her cigarette over the porch railing.

"Great. My sister's having a baby."

It was a stupid remark. Everyone laughed.

"Married, I presume?" Scott was grinning.

"Yes, for five years."

Silence. Margo could have kicked herself. She ought to give lessons on how to kill a conversation. "Well, I guess I'll go in." She was sure that was what everyone wanted. It was certainly what she wanted.

"You'll initial us in the book, won't you, Margo?" Eva asked.

"Okay."

"Margo's the best forger in the world. She can write B.J.'s and my initials in the curfew book better than we can do it ourselves," Eva explained to Scott. Then she turned back to Margo. "Hey, I forgot. Cricket and Stretch came around to ask you to a third floor party they're giving in their room tonight, as if you'd want to go." Eva laughed her throaty laugh. "Scott, you wouldn't believe this pair of roommates. One is about seven feet tall and the other . . ."

Eva was still rattling on as Margo pulled open the heavy oak door. Eva was right. She didn't want to go to a party, especially not at Cricket and Stretch's. She could just imagine who would be there, all the third floor misfits. Right now, all Margo wanted was to unpack and maybe watch some TV in the rec room.

"Hey, Margo." B.J. stuck her head in the door. "I

75

forgot to tell you that Miss Frye has been trying to reach you. She said to call her back."

"Thanks." That was more like it.

Margo didn't even take off her coat before she dialed Miss Frye's number on the pay phone down the hall from her room. She let it ring at least fifteen times before she hung up, which was ridiculous because Miss Frye's phone wasn't more than two or three rings away from anywhere in her apartment. Margo was surprised at how disappointed she felt. Maybe she had dialed the wrong number. She tried again, but with no luck.

"Hey, Margo."

Margo started. She hadn't heard anyone come up behind her. She spun around and almost tripped on her suitcase at the sight of the huge figure looming behind her in the dim light of the hall. But it was only Stretch, with a coke in one hand, a sloppy joe in the other, and a big smile on her face.

"We've been waiting for you to get back. Didn't Eva tell you Cricket and I are giving a third floor party and want you to come?"

Now Margo was caught. "I just this minute got in from New York," she hedged.

"Come on. We're having a ball."

Margo decided she might as well go. After all, she qualified as a misfit as much as anyone. "Thanks, Stretch. That sounds like fun."

She was right about the misfits. There were Cricket and Stretch, of course, and Armelia Ortiz, a Cuban refugee on scholarship who could hardly speak English, Barbara Glascock, the resident Haywood musical genius, Megan Barker, the dullest person Margo had ever met, and Mimi Denison, a stringy-haired girl who must have weighed two hundred pounds. But Dena Bickett and Jo Anne Rumery were a surprise. They were roommates, both black and both really popular. Dena was vice-president of student government and would probably be president next year, and Jo Anne ranked first in her class.

"Hi, Margo, you lucky dog, going to New York while we're stuck here."

"What about asking us next time? Yeah, baby, disco city here I come."

"Hey, Margo, since you don't live any place that you can think of, New York isn't a bad place to visit, right?"

Everyone laughed. Thunderstruck, Margo could hardly believe what she had heard. And it was Stretch who had said it. She was laughing too. Furious, Margo jumped up. There was no way she was going to stay and listen to this. Then she glanced around and saw that people were smiling, not in a mean way, but in a friendly, teasing way and she realized it was okay. They were kidding her to loosen her up. And they were right. As B.J. said, Margo knew she took herself too seriously. She managed a laugh.

"Yeah, this way I can pick and choose where I want to live."

"Here's to shipping off Durrett to New York permanently." Cricket raised her coke in a toast and everyone joined in with a "Hear. Hear."

"While you're at it, don't forget to ship off Mrs. Mifflin." Gym teacher.

"And Mrs. Kelly." The grumpy dining room superintendent.

"Amen to that."

"Listen, talking about Kelly, did you hear what she wants to do?" Stretch's expression was intense and Margo guessed she was about to launch into some crusade or other. Although they were off the subject of Miss Durrett, Margo knew total boredom was about to set in. But this time Stretch started on something Margo had already heard about from Eva and B.J. Mrs. Kelly wanted to change dining room procedure. Every student had dining room chores to do; the hardest one, like rinsing off dishes, was done by freshmen, next hardest by sophomores and so on up to the seniors, who did practically nothing. Now Kelly wanted to equalize the work load among all four years. Juniors like Eva and B.J. who had already put in their time were furious, and the seniors were in an uproar.

Stretch was opposed, too. "Those rules were worked out by student government and just because Kelly comes in as some new hotshot nutritionist doesn't mean she can overthrow established procedure. I think we ought to organize a strike."

Dena nodded agreement. "Student government meets next Tuesday night and we'll discuss it then."

"I'll tell Eva and B.J. what's up," Margo volunteered. "They're upset about this too and I know they'll pitch in."

Barbara Glascock gave a short snort of a laugh. It was the first sound she had made all evening.

"What's so funny?" Margo demanded, instantly defensive.

78

"You are, saying Eva and B.J. would pitch in. That'll be the day."

"I room with Eva and B.J. so I ought to know what they'll do or not do. The three of us are best friends."

Someone across the room snickered and when Margo looked over she saw it was Jo Anne. "Man, those two aren't best friends with anyone except maybe themselves."

All of a sudden, Margo sensed the room turn almost physically hostile as everyone nodded and murmured agreement.

"You're all just jealous." Margo hadn't meant to say that. The words just burst out. But it was true. Eva and B.J. had it all together and this group of misfits *was* jealous.

Jo Anne leaned forward and her eyes burned into Margo's. "If that's what you think, why don't you ask Barbara about it?"

Margo turned to Barbara. She was a solemn, mousy, brown-haired junior who was never known to be without her flute. Someone once told Margo that she even took it to bed with her. "Well?" Margo challenged.

Barbara's voice was low. "I was Eva's new girl roommate last year, didn't you know? Eva can't stand B.J.'s mess, so she always gets herself a new girl and lets B.J. room alone. That way they have eager fresh material every year to run their errands and cover up for them. The new girl who was Eva's roommate before me left at Christmas and never came back. I wasn't so lucky. My dad made me stick it out. It was the worst year I ever had. Now you're the winner in the Three Musketeers Sweepstakes. Good luck. You'll need it."

Margo stared in disbelief. She had never heard such lies. Sure, she covered up for Eva and B.J. sometimes, but she was glad to. It helped pay back for everything they had done for her. Why, Eva and B.J. had kept her on target on how to get along at Haywood so she wouldn't fall on her face like she usually did at a new school. Not only that, but Eva was the most savvy junior at Haywood, with the smartest-looking clothes, the best figure and the handsomest boy friend. And B.J. was the most beautiful girl Margo had ever seen and not in the least conceited about it either. No, Eva and B.J. were her friends and she needed them. Who could get along with Barbara anyway? She was about as interesting as a loaf of week-old bread, musical genius or no musical genius. Well, Margo didn't have to sit around and take this garbage.

She jumped up and brushed the crumbs off the new kilt she and Suzanne had picked out at Bloomingdale's this weekend. It was just like Eva's only a different plaid.

"Thanks a lot, Cricket. I have to go. I'm not even unpacked yet. Thanks, Stretch, see you."

Margo was already on her way down the hall when Cricket came hurrying after her. "Wait, Margo, don't be mad. I want to talk to you."

Margo shook her head without turning around and kept on going. "I can't, Cricket. I have homework to do."

It was her own fault. Eva had warned her about that group and she should have listened.

eleven

If only Margo had English First period instead of
Eighth, she'd have gotten the whole thing over with.
As it was, she had the entire day to stew about it, and
to make matters worse, this ridiculous fear she had
of speaking up in English was beginning to affect her
other classes too. It was like some kind of infectious
disease. Even her classmates were beginning to dread
having teachers call on her. And Margo wasn't having
that easy a time of it that she could afford to let
anything pull her marks down.

Then Margo learned a trick. If she had what she
wanted to say all blocked out mentally and volun-

teered the answer, she could get through it. Not terrifically, but passably. Otherwise, if she were called on unexpectedly, she really botched it up. So Margo did her homework carefully and made an effort to volunteer every chance she could. Except in English. In English, all she could do was sit in frozen terror.

Miss Frye and Saturday tennis were Margo's salvation. She looked forward to it all week as her pocket of sanity. On the third Saturday in October, Miss Frye picked Margo up as usual. On their way to Greenbrook Club, they talked about Haywood's upcoming match with the Stonecroft School.

"We ought to beat them easily, Allie. I don't know anything about their new coach, but we haven't lost a match to Stonecroft in two years. I hear their third singles is hot at net but weak at the baseline. You'll just have to keep her back." Miss Frye was concentrating on her driving, but had time to reach over and give Margo an encouraging pat.

Margo nodded. "I wish my own net game were stronger."

"At least it's improving. We'll work on it today." Miss Frye braked the jeep in the club parking lot, started to get out, then groaned. "Will you look at that? The men must be having some kind of tournament."

Sure enough, all the courts were taken and fifteen or twenty middle-aged men were sitting around watching the matches. "That's okay, Miss Frye. I don't mind waiting," Margo said. Besides, maybe she'd see that redheaded Pete Montgomery.

Miss Frye tapped her fingers on the steering wheel

in annoyance. "The Board of Governors has got to do something about this. Men only until noon is bad enough, but now their tournaments are running into the afternoon. I refuse to sit around while my blood pressure soars. If you don't mind, Allie, I'll leave you here and get some errands done. I'll be back in about an hour."

Margo opened the jeep door. "Sure, that's fine with me, Miss Frye." Truthfully, it couldn't have been better. Margo had spotted Pete playing doubles with three older men on the middle court.

It was pleasant sitting in the sun. The October days had gotten cool enough to wear a warm-up suit, but now Margo took off her jacket, half closed her eyes and raised her face to the sun's rays. She wanted to watch Pete without his knowing it.

He was playing much better today, not so wild, and she could see right away he was playing to his opponents' weaknesses. Margo tried to figure out the score but the server wasn't calling it out the way he should have. Then all of a sudden, everyone looked tense and determined and Pete's opponents started to play cautiously. Margo figured it must be close to match point for Pete and his partner. Deuce, then add, then deuce again. The score seesawed back and forth about ten times. Now Margo was sitting up straight with all pretense of not watching forgotten. Most of the men on the sidelines were watching too. Wham, Pete smashed a deadly overhead at his opponent's feet and the match was won. To a smattering of applause, the four of them shook hands, all smiles now and pleasant remarks.

83

Pete threw a sweatshirt over his shoulders and waved to Margo. She was sure he had known all along that she was there and probably, she realized, he had been playing to her. Margo waved back as he walked toward her. He was almost a comical figure with his skinny bowed legs and unruly red hair. He wore an old T-shirt and shorts with the hem hanging down. Margo couldn't help wondering what Eva and B.J. would think of him.

"Hi, Allie." There was certainly nothing wrong with his grin. It practically split his face from ear to ear. And she was pleased he called her Allie. Miss Frye was the only other person who called her that, which gave it an especially nice connotation.

"Where's Miss Frye?" Pete picked up a towel and wiped off his face first and then his racket handle.

"She had some errands in town. She'll be back in half an hour or so."

"Come on and hit some balls with me until she gets here," Pete leaned down and whispered in Margo's ear. "These old geezers didn't even warm me up."

Margo laughed and stood up. She had hoped Pete would ask her to play. She knew she couldn't beat him, but he had a terrific topspin on his shots and she wanted to see if she could handle it.

They rallied for a while and at first Margo couldn't do anything with Pete's topspin at all. Then she began to get the hang of it. "Let's play a couple of games," she called across the net. The sun was warming overhead and now that they had hit a few, she was beginning to feel good and loose.

"You serve." Pete lobbed the balls over the net to her.

Pete won the first three games easily. Then, as Margo began to get a feel for his game, she started to do better. She won the next game to bring the score up to 3-1, then took the lead in the fifth game. But Pete tied it up at deuce. It was a close game. The advantage went back and forth with neither of them able to win. Then, as Margo walked over to the fence to retrieve a stray ball, she saw Miss Frye standing by the gate watching them. Margo had no idea how long she'd been there, but she was frowning.

"Hi, Miss Frye. I didn't know you were back. As soon as I win the next two points, the game will be over."

Pete must have heard from his side of the court. "As soon as *I* win the next two points, the game will be over."

"Don't hurry on my account." Miss Frye's usually soft voice was brisk.

Maybe, Margo decided, it was time to stop. "That's okay, Miss Frye, we can quit now, really. We were just hitting some balls so it's no big deal. Hey, Pete," she called, "I'm going to stop now."

Pete, who was already in position to receive service, looked puzzled. "Come on, Allie, you can't give up now."

Margo walked over to pick up her warm-up suit from where she'd left it on the net post. "Miss Frye is waiting for me. We can finish the set some other time."

Pete followed her through the gate. "Forget finishing it. That was game, set, match for Mr. Peter Montgomery, won by default."

Startled, Margo turned around. But Pete was grinning and she realized he was only kidding and not really angry. She laughed and glanced at Miss Frye, expecting her to be laughing too. But Miss Frye was busy taking the cover off her racket and must not have heard. At least she didn't seem amused.

twelve

On the day of Haywood's tennis match against Stonecroft, Margo was more uptight than usual in English. She was sure Miss Durrett would pick that day to call on her. Miss Durrett wasn't stupid. She knew Margo had a match that afternoon and she also knew if anything could botch up her game, being called on in English would do it. But Miss Durrett never looked at Margo the whole period.

It was a perfect October day for tennis, a little cool but with no breeze at all. Now that the days were getting shorter, the sun sometimes sank low enough in the west to be a nuisance, but this afternoon the leaden sky was overcast. All in all, just-right playing conditions, and with Haywood's previous record against Stonecroft, everyone on the team was confident of winning.

So when Margo started playing her match, she couldn't believe what she was up against. Her opponent, Joan Something-or-other, had beautiful strokes and a killing backhand. She was about five feet ten, and Margo watched in horror as she gobbled up the court in long, graceful strides. And her net game was deadly, with almost every return a putaway. Their match lasted two hours. Margo fought for every point, trying desperately to keep her opponent in the back court. Whenever Joan made it to net, she invariably won the point.

Margo was only vaguely aware of what the other teams were doing. Two of Haywood's doubles teams had gone to Stonecroft to play on their courts while the other four teams had stayed at Haywood. Izzy at second singles finished her match after about an hour, then Phoebe and Hope playing first doubles were done, then Trish at first singles finished. Margo was concentrating so hard on her own game, she had no idea what their scores were. At last her match was over and she had lost in three sets.

It wasn't until they had shaken hands and walked off the court that Margo realized the whole Haywood team was sitting on the grass watching her, even the two doubles teams who had gone to Stonecroft to play. That meant they had finished and already come back. Everyone looked dejected. Margo didn't blame them. She had let Miss Frye and the whole team down. Stonecroft was supposed to be such a pushover and here she'd gone and lost Haywood's first match against them in two years.

Then, unbelievably, Miss Frye rushed over with a big grin on her face and shook Margo's hand. "Allie, you played brilliantly. I never saw you play better." She lowered her voice so Joan couldn't hear. "You shouldn't feel bad about losing. That girl you played is a ringer. When they heard what a strong player you are, they moved her down from second singles to third."

Before Margo could even apologize, Miss Frye had walked over to say goodbye to the Stonecroft coach.

"What were the other scores?" Margo put on her jacket and sat down on the grass with the rest of the team.

"We all lost." That was Dinah, a member of the fourth doubles team who had played on the Stonecroft courts.

"All?" Margo couldn't believe it. Stonecroft was supposed to have such a weak team.

"All," Dinah repeated.

It was a real conversation stopper. The whole team was silent as they watched the Stonecroft coach triumphantly herd her players into their school van and take off down the driveway. Miss Frye waved a cordial goodbye, then turned and walked back to where the team waited. When Margo saw her expression, goosebumps prickled her arms and she instinctively zipped up her jacket.

Because everyone was still seated on the ground, Miss Frye seemed to tower above them. "I don't want to hear one excuse, not one. You were terrible, all of you, with the exception of Allie. I can't tell you how disappointed I am in the rest of you."

"She lost too." Trish mumbled under her breath. Margo was sitting next to Trish and heard the remark though she was sure Miss Frye hadn't. Margo wished she had. Trish was right. She had lost. This was no time to single her out as special.

But Miss Frye wasn't finished. She turned on Trish. "You totally lost your concentration, Trish. I never saw you make so many errors. Izzy, you were even worse. I sensed you giving up before the first set was over. As for Phoebe and Hope at first doubles, you two acted as if you'd never played together before. Second doubles was no better. What third and fourth doubles did over at Stonecroft, I can only imagine from your scores. I saw one fighter out there, Allie. If the rest of you had fought as hard, I would have been proud no matter what the scores were. As it is, I feel you've all let me down."

With that, Miss Frye turned on her heel and stalked down the driveway to her jeep. She got in, slammed the door and took off in a burst of exhaust fumes. The team sat in stunned silence. Margo would never have imagined that Miss Frye could be so cutting. And to humiliate Trish and Izzy and Phoebe and Hope like that in front of everyone. She turned to Trish. "Hey, I'm sorry . . ."

"Don't be sorry," Trish snapped. "Frye's in your hip pocket so what's to be sorry about?" She jumped up, brushed off her warm-up suit, then reached down and pulled Izzy to her feet. Phoebe stood up too.

"Wait a minute, that's not fair . . ."

But Trish and Izzy and Phoebe had already picked up their rackets and walked away without letting Margo finish.

It was like a signal. Everyone else got up too. No one said anything as they gathered up their rackets and towels and sweaters and started across the grass toward the driveway. No one spoke to Margo or even looked at her. But she hadn't done anything. She ran after Dinah and grabbed Dinah's arm.

"Dinah, wait for me."

Dinah stopped and turned around, but didn't answer. She had an open, friendly face like a puppy's, only now it looked as if it had been whipped.

"I didn't ask Miss Frye to stick up for me." Margo heard a whine in her voice but she couldn't help it. "I just played the best I could. Now everyone's treating me as if I had done something terrible."

Dinah shrugged. "Trish and Izzy and Phoebe are the big guns of the team. When they get mad at someone, the whole team gets mad."

"I didn't do anything to them."

Dinah gave a short bark of a laugh. "Maybe you didn't, but Miss Frye did. When she put you at third singles that moved Phoebe down to first doubles. It was the end of a beautiful friendship. Trish, Izzy and Phoebe have been Haywood's big singles threesome for a long time. The school newspaper even called them the TIPtops. Get it? Their initials spell TIP. Then you came along and all of a sudden, they weren't the TIPtops any more. So you can see why they're not exactly thrilled."

Of course. Margo should have realized that was the reason why the tennis team, especially the seniors, had been so antagonistic toward her, but she hadn't seen beyond the glory of playing third singles. Margo watched Dinah run down the driveway to catch up with the others. She didn't even try to follow. All of a sudden she was too tired to do anything. It had been a long, hard match, and right now having the whole team angry at her was more than she could handle. Miss Frye was trying to help, but she just didn't understand. Putting Margo in Phoebe's position, plus holding her up as an example, was killing her with the rest of the team.

Margo felt a drop of rain on her hand. Another drop hit her face. She looked up at the gray clouds massed overhead. Let it rain. Let it pour. Maybe she'd get soaking wet and catch pneumonia. It would be a perfect solution. No more Durrett, no more tennis team. Yes, a good bout of pneumonia would suit Margo fine right now.

thirteen

As Margo came out of her room the next morning
to go to breakfast, she saw Trish and Izzy and Phoebe
coming down the hall from the opposite direction.
She smiled tentatively, started to speak, then stopped
and waited for them to say something first. But their
eyes went right through and past her. It was such a
total cut it was almost a physical blow. With her heart
racing, she paused by the stair railing to let them get
ahead of her. She watched the three figures go down
the stairs, getting smaller and smaller. Or maybe it
was she who was getting smaller and smaller. Maybe
she would just fade away until she didn't exist at all.

Certainly Trish and Izzy and Phoebe had acted as if she didn't exist.

By the time Margo reached the dining room, the doors were just closing. She had to hurry to get in, then wondered why she had bothered. For once she didn't feel like eating. But Cricket and Stretch who must have seen her standing by the door, waved her over to their practically empty table. As she sat down, she wished that Eva and B.J. were there. They'd have laughed and said Trish and Izzy and Phoebe didn't amount to anything, that Trish's father owned a two-bit drugstore in Indiana, for God's sake, and Izzy's father was a wheeler dealer millionaire who had somehow finagled Izzy a full scholarship. As for Phoebe, she came from a family of nine children, if that wasn't the pits. But Margo didn't have Eva and B.J. All she had were Cricket and Stretch, who spent the meal laughing over the antics of the hamster Stretch had smuggled into their room last week.

The incident with Trish and Izzy and Phoebe bothered Margo all day. It had been so important to her that the tennis team be her friends. Now, with those three seniors pulling the strings, practically the only one who would speak to her was Dinah. Maybe that was why her guard was down in English. Miss Durrett had been talking nonstop about grammar for almost the entire period. Margo was half listening and half watching a Lower School soccer game out the window when she heard that familiar raspy voice. "Well, Allinger?"

Allinger, that was her. Margo jumped to her feet so fast the blood rushed from her head and she felt dizzy. Maybe it was the lightheadedness that did it, but all of a sudden Margo felt disconnected from the Allinger that was her. It was like being two separate entities, with the real Allinger watching the unreal Allinger. It was a disappointing sight. The unreal Allinger wasn't much. In fact, the unreal Allinger was a flop, a flop in class, a flop at making friends, a flop in every way.

Vaguely Margo was aware of Miss Durrett smiling that tight thin smile from her position on her desk. It was a smile so superior, so confident of victory, that it might have been a signal flag waving. Miss Durrett glanced down at the register book in her lap.

"I didn't realize how long it's been since I've called on you, Allinger. We'll have to make up for my oversight. Please diagram all the sentences on pages 110 and 111 orally and explain the grammar behind your reasoning."

Margo picked up her book, opened to page 110 and looked at it. The words made no more sense than a page of Chinese symbols. There was no way she could read it. As she continued to stare at her book, she became aware of the silence, that familiar heavy silence urgent with tension, with no one looking at Margo and no one looking at Miss Durrett either. Margo heard the sounds of the soccer game outside, the kids shouting, the whistle blowing. That was reality. This stuffy little classroom was only illusion.

As the sounds from outside swelled and filled her head, Margo felt herself floating. Now she was looking down not only on herself, but on the whole room as well, seeing everything in a way she had never seen it before—the dark streak running along the part in Miss Durrett's blond hair, Liz Thomas polishing her nails under cover of her desk top, the package of cigarillos in Jennifer Katz's book bag.

The real Allinger rose still higher. The classroom faded and now she was overlooking the green patch that was the school soccer field just the way she had watched Trish and Izzy and Phoebe go downstairs this morning getting smaller and smaller. Even Haywood itself was Lilliputian, a miniature fortress with its little cone-shaped tower and its winding ribbon of a driveway. It was pleasant. Up here there were no Miss Durretts or staring classmates or sentences to be diagramed. All that was behind her as she floated free . . . free . . .

"Allinger, sit down!"

Allinger. The name registered. The real Allinger clicked together with the unreal Allinger like a key fitting a lock. Margo was back in the classroom with its heat of accumulated bodies and its dead-chalk smell. She looked up and saw Miss Durrett still seated on her desk. Miss Durrett's pale face was blotchy and her mouth was a grim line. Usually Miss Durrett kept her face expressionless, but now she was obviously furious.

As Margo sat down, someone giggled. Someone else joined in. Cricket was smiling, too, and when she caught Margo's eye, she winked. The whole class was in a state of suppressed glee, nudging each other and exchanging amused glances. It took Margo a moment to realize the class wasn't laughing at her, they were laughing at Miss Durrett. Margo had

96

bested her. In some unknown, unplanned way, Margo had beaten Miss Durrett.

"I want to talk to you after class, Allinger. And since you seem to be enjoying yourself so much, Jones, suppose you diagram pages 110 and 111." Miss Durrett practically trembled with the effort of controlling her anger.

Cricket gave Margo's arm a quick squeeze as she passed on her way out at the end of the period. "Watch yourself," she warned.

There didn't seem to be much to watch. Miss Durrett had apparently forgotten all about her. Margo waited in her seat while Miss Durrett fiddled around her desk, rearranged papers, checked over lists, wrote in her notebook, all without so much as glancing at Margo. Then she spoke, though she still didn't look up.

"We seem to be dealing with a serious problem here, Allinger."

She made it sound like a question. "Yes," Margo agreed.

"What do you think the solution is?"

All of a sudden, Margo was consumed by a blood-red rush of hatred. She hated Miss Durrett. She had never hated anyone so much in her whole life. And she knew as surely as if the words had been spoken aloud that Miss Durrett hated her. The hatred between them was like a moving body of water. Margo was drowning in it and the current wouldn't even let her come up for air. She was being swept downstream, dragged past friends, schoolwork, even her tennis. She shook her head. "I don't know."

"You could ask to be transferred to another English class." Still that blond head was down.

Margo had thought of that. Eva had even suggested it. But it was too late. What Miss Durrett had done to her had poisoned all her classes, not just English. Every day it was getting harder to speak up in class, any class. Margo was setting her alarm earlier and earlier so she had more time to go over each day's work to prepare herself. No, transferring wouldn't help. And in the back of her mind, only half articulated to herself, Margo knew if she transferred Miss Durrett had won the whole ball game. What Miss Durrett wanted was a public triumph, and if Margo asked to be transferred out of her class, that was what she would get.

"No." Margo's voice came out surprisingly strong.

Miss Durrett's head snapped up. Probably Miss Durrett hadn't expected that. Probably Miss Durrett had expected Margo to jump at the opportunity. Now Miss Durrett studied Margo intently as if to figure out her next move. After a moment, she stood up, limped around to the front of her desk and leaned against it. Margo couldn't help looking at Miss Durrett's legs. And she was sure Miss Durrett knew she was looking. It was as if Miss Durrett were using her crippled legs as a weapon, as if to say, Look, I can defeat you whether or not you've got two good legs and I haven't. It occurred to Margo that Miss Durrett always wore a skirt that showed her legs, rather than slacks, not only to flaunt her disability, but to manipulate people with it as well.

Miss Durrett folded her arms over her chest.

"There's a good psychologist in town that Haywood uses for referrals. I think you should consider getting professional help."

Lots of people went to psychiatrists. Margo knew two girls from her last school who used to brag about it. Margo didn't mind going. She was sinking, she knew that, and she knew a psychologist could probably help her. But she would never go at Miss Durrett's suggestion. Not ever. That would be even more of a triumph for Miss Durrett than if Margo transferred out of her class.

Margo shook her head and forced herself not to break the eye contact between them. "No," she said again.

It was Miss Durrett who severed the connection. She turned around abruptly and began to gather up her books. "Then that just about covers the possibilities, doesn't it, Allinger? I'll see you in class tomorrow."

That was it. Margo was trapped for the whole year. Miss Durrett had given her a chance to be free and Margo had turned it down. It was strange. Miss Durrett should have felt great and Margo should have felt terrible. But Margo had gotten a glimpse of Miss Durrett's face before she turned her back and it was crimson with anger and frustration. As for Margo, she didn't feel terrible at all. She felt a sudden surge of joy course through her. In some way she didn't understand, she had duelled with Miss Durrett for the second time that day, and won.

fourteen

"It's all set, Margo." Eva had just come back into the room after a long phone call with Scott. "Roger is coming over on Saturday with Scott and Gavin and the six of us will spend the day together."

Margo put down her calculator and looked up in dismay. She was having a hard time with her Math homework, but now all thoughts of Math fled as she pictured Scott and Gavin, good-looking, witty, sophisticated seniors. Roger, who was Scott's roommate, was probably even more so. Margo already knew he had been kicked out of two schools and kept an illegal car off campus.

100

"Eva, you shouldn't have. I can't. I'm busy. I play tennis on Saturday with Miss Frye . . ."

"It's too late. I had a hard enough time . . ." Eva cut herself off in mid-sentence. "Listen, it'll be great. Roger is terrific, believe me, and he's dying to meet you."

Roger was probably dying to meet Margo like he was dying to break his leg. "Can't you get someone else? He'd never know the difference," Margo pleaded.

"We're the Three Musketeers, Margo, you know that, and we stick together. Besides, who else is there?" Eva looked annoyed. Little frown lines creased her forehead.

Margo tried, but she couldn't come up with the name of one single girl. Anyone Eva and B.J. might find acceptable already had a boy friend, and anyone else she could think of, Eva and B.J. wouldn't want.

"Let me think about it, Eva," she hedged.

Eva smiled as if it were all settled. "We'll have a blast."

Then on Thursday, after the Haywood tennis team had soundly trounced Mott-Smith Academy, Miss Frye came up and put her hand on Margo's shoulder. She was in a really good mood, happy, smiling and kidding around with everyone. "Good game, Allie. The whole team did a great job today. Now we're back on the right track." She started to go, then turned back. "By the way, I won't be able to make our Saturday tennis this week. I have to spend the afternoon at the dentist having a root canal job done that's going to be murder. Sorry about that."

It was like fate. Margo was destined to have that

date with Roger whether she wanted it or not.

But when she and Eva came downstairs and Margo saw Roger in the front hall with Scott, her first impulse was to turn around and run back up. Eva had said Roger was eighteen but he looked at least twenty, and not only was he handsome, with black hair and dark eyes, he had a mustache as well. There was no way Margo could think of anything to say to someone with a mustache. She heard herself clump loudly down the stairs. Eva had helped put her outfit together, her new plaid kilt, a turtleneck under a Shetland sweater, and a borrowed pair of Eva's boots. But the boots were a size too big and even with socks underneath, they felt as big as gunboats.

Eva gave Scott a big hug and a kiss right in the middle of Big Hall. Margo didn't know where to look or what to do with her hands. Roger grinned at her as if to communicate that he knew what she was thinking. Eva wiggled out of Scott's arms and pulled Margo over. "Margo, this is Roger Munson. Roger, I want you to meet Margo Allinger, a roommate to end all roommates."

"Hi, Margo Allinger."

It was funny. One minute Roger was looking right into Margo's eyes, and the next his glance had slid over her shoulder. Margo turned around. Two good-looking seniors whose names she didn't know were coming down the stairs. As soon as they realized Roger had noticed them, they put on a big show of laughing and talking. They kept up their act all the way across Big Hall with Roger watching the entire performance. Only when they had gone out the front door did he turn back to Margo.

The four of them talked about nothing in particular for a few minutes, then started out for the stables. Because B.J.'s horse was sick, she had spent the morning at the stables where Gavin had met her. Now they were all going to get together. Margo hoped Roger hadn't brought his illegal car. She knew she was square, but she didn't want to ride in it. Luckily, the problem never came up. Roger had driven his car over but parked it in town.

With Eva and Scott leading the way and Margo and Roger following, the four of them walked the half mile to the stables. Margo wished their order of parade had been reversed. Eva and Scott strolled along with their arms around each other, whispering and occasionally kissing. Margo was embarrassed into silence, but it didn't seem to bother Roger at all. He picked up a stick and used it as a walking cane, humming along under his breath.

"Do you play tennis, Roger?" It was the only dumb remark Margo could come up with.

"I've tried it a couple of times but it's too much of a sweat sport for me. Now golf, there's a game." Roger swung his walking stick like a golf club.

What a relief. Margo could have cared less about golf but she clutched at the subject just to fill the empty spaces. Roger was a three-handicap player, had won trophies and played in amateur tournaments all over the east. Roger's golf carried them the rest of the way.

Then they were at the stables looking for B.J. and Gavin. It was Eva who found them down by the riding ring. Margo watched the three of them walk down the dark stable corridor toward her as the

103

bright sunlight at their backs threw them into silhouette. For the first time, Margo realized how pigeon-toed B.J. was and what terrible posture she had. Then Margo had to smile. She should be so pigeon-toed and have such terrible posture. Even with her hair pulled back in a scarf and wearing beat-up old boots and grubby jeans, B.J. was spectacular-looking. Eva was outlined against the light, too. Eva had a great figure, good legs and beautiful posture. Her clothes and hair were always perfect, and yet it was B.J. who got all the stares and admiring glances. Margo had never thought about it before, but that must have been hard on Eva, who cared so much about her appearance. But Eva didn't seem to mind. That, Margo decided, was what being a friend meant.

By the time B.J. showered and changed, everyone was famished. The six of them headed for town for some hamburgers. And beer. When the waitress took their orders, all three boys pulled out ID cards for identification and to Margo's amazement, so did Eva and B.J. Then they all looked expectantly at Margo. She tried to cover up by saying she had lost hers, but she didn't think anyone believed her. It didn't matter. She didn't like beer anyway.

The day went into blocks of time. A block for lunch, then a block of errands that Eva insisted on doing, then a block of playing frisbee in the park, then a block of hitting out golf balls at the driving range. Though Margo wasn't very good at golf, Eva was worse. Scott solved that by putting his arms around her and giving her a golf lesson. Of sorts. Though B.J. was doing fine on her own, Gavin took his cue from Scott and gave B.J. an arms-around lesson too. Not Roger. He just smacked ball after ball a million miles out into the field. Margo could have wrapped the club around her neck and he wouldn't have noticed. Finally, she gave up and just sat down on a bench to watch.

She realized that the girl behind the ticket counter was watching too. Margo didn't blame her. Roger was really good-looking, with his tight curly black hair cut short, and a bump on his nose as if it had once been broken that was somehow appealing. He waved at Margo on his way to buy another bucket of balls. He seemed to be gone a long time. When Margo glanced over, she saw him talking and kidding around with the girl behind the counter as if they knew each other. Margo watched them laugh and flirt and couldn't help feeling down. She wasn't beautiful like B.J. and she wasn't clever like Eva. She wasn't even smart like Cricket. She was just herself, as much of a flop with a date as she was with everything else.

Then it began to get cold and they were walking back to Haywood. Margo plunged her hands in her blazer pockets just to have something to do with them as she listened to plans for the evening—a spaghetti dinner at Mario's, then a stop at Charlie's Disco or maybe Gasoline Alley. Roger didn't say a word until they reached the front porch of Big Hall. The other four moved away as if it were prearranged.

"Eva probably told you I have to pick up my sister at the Philadelphia Airport tonight. I'm sorry, Margo, but I've got to be shoving off."

For the first time that day, Roger seemed ill at ease.

Margo didn't blame him. The story was such an obvious lie that even gullible she saw through it. Probably, she thought, he was meeting that girl from the driving range as soon as he dumped her. In one way, Margo minded terribly. Roger's lie just confirmed her own opinion of herself. In another way, she didn't mind at all. Truthfully, she wasn't having any better time than Roger was, and there wasn't one more subject she could dredge up to keep the conversation going.

"Sure, I understand, Roger. That's okay. And thanks a lot. I had a great time."

Roger's look of relief that he was off the hook so easily was almost comical. He stuck out his hand and for the first time since they met, he looked her right in the eye and smiled. "Hey, listen, have a great year, Margo, and I'll be seeing you."

Roger waved to the others and loped down the driveway. Margo watched him go. He was everything any girl would want in a boy—tall, handsome, a good athlete and funny, too, when he wanted to be. The trouble was, Margo didn't like him. And she didn't know why. Certainly she had never felt relaxed with him the way she did with Pete Montgomery. But then she had never done anything more with Pete than hit a few tennis balls. Maybe something was wrong with her that she couldn't be herself with boys.

All of a sudden she was totally and completely exhausted. She said goodbye to everyone and headed for her room. She didn't even care whether Roger met up with them later or not. She was so tired she could hardly drag herself up the stairs, and Eva's boots felt like ten-pound weights on her feet.

"Hey, Margo, phone."

Margo picked up the receiver.

"Allie?" It was Miss Frye. "I'm not doing a thing tonight and I feel like celebrating getting that root canal job done. I'd love to have you join me for dinner, just some spaghetti and a salad. Then the two of us can go see that French movie in town that's supposed to be so funny. How does that sound?"

Miss Frye's invitation was like a sea breeze on a hot day. It swept all of Margo's tension and exhaustion away, and she felt like a million. The evening sounded perfect was how it sounded. "I'd love to, Miss Frye. I'm not doing a thing either."

fifteen

Every Friday morning the school had assembly in Kurt Hall right after breakfast. Mrs. Singleton, the headmistress, always led the flag salute, "The Star-Spangled Banner," the school song, and then readings from the Old and New Testaments. Back when Julia Brett Haywood opened her classes for 'genteel young females,' Haywood had been a church school and in a way it still was. At least there was a perfunctory grace before dinner every night, as well as Wednesday chapel services which no one ever went to, plus the Bible readings on Fridays.

And Friday assembly included announcements about club activities, student government decisions, a report on the past week's sports, and what events were taking place over the weekend. The first Friday in November, Eva was to make an announcement about a poetry reading scheduled for the following Sunday afternoon. The night before, she had casually mentioned to Margo that she planned to recite a poem she had written to spark interest in the program. Margo couldn't believe it. The thought of having to make an announcement would have paralyzed her, but Eva acted as if she were looking forward to it.

Margo usually sat with Cricket and Stretch way over on the left of Kurt Hall. Over the past weeks, Cricket and Stretch had gotten in the habit of stopping by her room to pick her up for breakfast. Then on Fridays, they just naturally drifted into assembly together. As soon as Margo settled in her seat between Stretch and Cricket, she looked up at the stage. The seniors were finding their places and getting settled, too. For assembly, the whole school dressed in uniform, and the seniors, in their yellow blazers, sat on the stage. Every class had a class color and this year's seniors had gotten stuck with yellow. From a distance, the stage looked like a field of bright daffodils, but close up, Margo knew most of the blazers were pretty grubby. Luckily, Margo's class color was forest green.

Then Margo saw Eva take her seat on the stage, next to last in the line of announcement chairs. She looked completely at ease as she pulled out a hairbrush and unobtrusively brushed her shiny dark hair. She was smiling as if she were enjoying the experience. Enjoying it! Eva was amazing.

For some reason the Bible passages Mrs. Singleton

read were longer than usual and Margo sensed Cricket to her right getting fidgety. Finally Cricket pulled out a scratch pad, scribbled a note and passed it to Margo, indicating that Margo should read it and pass it on to Stretch.

'This time I'm going to take action,' the note said. 'I will not sit through this one more Friday.'

It was as if the note were in code. Margo had no idea what Cricket was talking about. But Stretch seemed to know. She nodded vigorously in agreement, took out her pen and scrawled along the bottom of the paper, 'I couldn't agree with you more.' and passed it back to Cricket.

At last Mrs. Singleton was finished. Announcements came next. Trish and her tennis announcements were third in line. Margo had never thought about tennis announcements before, but as she listened to Trish read through who won what match and what the team standing in the league was, her heart began to race in that panicky way. Margo was the best sophomore player on the team and in two years, she'd probably be captain. That meant she'd be standing up there making announcements every Friday.

Margo studied the rows of seniors seated on the stage. Their chairs faced the podium, so they were all looking directly at Trish. Margo turned around in her seat and glanced back at the assembled school. Every eye was watching Trish. Every ear was listening. Hundreds and hundreds of eyes and ears. It was terrifying. Margo could never get up on that stage and speak before the entire school. Not now, not in two years.

110

She shook her head to clear it. She was going off the deep end. Two years from now, some new hotshot player might be captain, or the school might have burned down or World War III might have started. She had enough problems right now without projecting worries two years into the future. Just to distract herself, she played a game of looking around Kurt Hall to try and match names with faces. It was a mistake. Practically the first person she saw was Miss Durrett in the teachers' section. Miss Durrett had a little smile on her lips and her pointy chin was stuck up in the air in her usual arrogant pose. Miss Durrett. The Enemy. Miss Durrett hadn't called on Margo in two weeks. Margo hadn't let her guard down that whole time and Miss Durrett must have known it. She apparently called on Margo only when she could catch Margo unawares. It was an endless cat-and-mouse game between them.

Now it was Eva's turn at the podium. Cricket and Stretch were still passing notes back and forth, but Margo's attention was riveted on the stage. When Eva's name was called, she stood up, hesitated a moment, then walked slowly across the platform. When she reached the podium, she hesitated again, then flipped her long hair back from her face and smiled out at the audience. Margo would have given anything to have that kind of assurance. Then Margo forgot everything as she was caught up in Eva's performance. Instead of making the announcement first, she opened with her poem, reciting it slowly and dramatically without any notes. For once even the coughing and restlessness ceased as she hooked the whole audience. Eva was terrific and she was Margo's roommate. Margo was so proud of her she sat up straighter, as if some of the admiration Eva was getting might rub off on her.

Cricket and Stretch were still muttering and complaining as they all marched out of Kurt Hall. Right away Margo looked for Eva, to congratulate her, to be seen with her so everyone would know they were roommates and best friends. *Margo Allinger must be okay if she's Eva Gordon's best friend.*

"Don't you think so, Margo?"

Cricket, all seriousness, had asked a question Margo hadn't heard.

"Think what?"

There was Eva over by the door talking to Mr. Schultz, the drama coach. They were deep in conversation.

"Don't you think it's time we did something about the Bible readings?"

Although Stretch nodded agreement, Margo still didn't know what Cricket was talking about. "What about them?"

"There are a couple of possibilities." Cricket ticked them off on her fingers. "Those of us who object, like Janie Levy, Ghana Greene, Jo Anne Rumery, me, and the others, could probably be excused, but that doesn't solve the basic problem. I think the Bible readings and hymns should be eliminated altogether. I've already spoken to Mrs. Singleton and gotten nowhere. Now I think we ought to go to the student government about it."

"But Cricket, this is a church school and a private school, too. Can't they do anything they want?"

112

Margo couldn't believe it was the Bible readings that Cricket and Stretch were so whipped up about. No one listened anyway. Besides, Margo knew Stretch went to the Presbyterian Church every Sunday and was active in their youth fellowship program. There was no reason for her to get involved in this.

It was as if Stretch read Margo's mind. She leaned down from her towering height and her expression was as serious as Cricket's. "It doesn't matter whether I'm Presbyterian, Buddhist or whatever. When Cricket or anyone else's rights are violated, mine are too. I have to get involved."

For the first time, Margo was listening, really listening. Don't do it, she wanted to say. Cricket and Stretch. Mutt and Jeff. You're already the laughing stock of the school, just like me, the girl who can't get two words out of her mouth in succession. Don't make it worse. Just play it low-key and maybe someday people will come to accept us.

"So how about it, Margo, can we count on your support?"

Margo just stared at Cricket. All the things she wanted to say never came out. They just stayed inside her, all bottled up. No, they couldn't count on her support. She couldn't handle any more hassle. She was having a hard enough time keeping her head above water as it was.

Out of the corner of her eye, Margo saw Eva say goodbye to Mr. Schultz and start toward the front door of Big Hall. B.J. was with her and they were laughing about something.

"I'll see you later, Cricket. I have to hurry." Margo

started to run to catch up to Eva and B.J. They wouldn't involve her in a hassle. They knew enough not to go looking for trouble. Best friends, that's what they were.

"Hey, Eva, B.J. Wait for me," Margo called.

But they must not have heard her. They kept right on going.

sixteen

That week was one of the loveliest weeks of the fall, real November Indian summer, with more warm weather predicted for the weekend. That was fine with Margo. Her blood must have thinned out living in California so that she didn't care if winter ever set in. Though the good weather had prolonged the outdoor tennis season, that Friday Miss Frye had cancelled practice. She was flying out to Chicago for the weekend to visit her father.

Having Miss Frye gone until Monday left Margo at loose ends. Saturdays with Miss Frye were what she looked forward to most. The Saturday morning tennis was not only improving her game, but it was fun too. Saturday afternoons were lazy. After lunch, she and Miss Frye sometimes went into Philadelphia to a museum or art show or movie, but most of the time they stayed in the apartment listening to the stereo and playing backgammon.

Now a deadly weekend loomed ahead. Eva and B.J. were going to a Lewiston dance with Scott and Gavin and wouldn't be back until Sunday night. Margo had even called Suzanne to ask if she could come visit, but Suzanne and Don planned to be away for the weekend. All of which left Margo hanging around Saturday morning watching Eva and B.J. pack, and trying to think of an excuse not to go shopping in Philadelphia with Cricket and Stretch.

"Caller at the front desk for Room 36," someone yelled from down the hall.

Room 36 was their room.

"That must be Scott and Gavin." Eva sounded annoyed. "They're more than an hour early. I'll go down and tell them they'll have to wait."

Eva was back in a minute. It wasn't Scott and Gavin. It was a visitor for Margo. "Bjorn Borg awaits you, Margo, all five feet two of him and ready for Wimbledon." Eva laughed. "Where did you ever pick him up?"

It must be Pete Montgomery. Margo blushed. "I've seen him over at Greenbrook Club a couple of times."

"He looks more your type, B.J. He's so bowlegged he must have spent his life on horseback." Eva laughed again.

"Pete's okay. He's not so bad." Now why did Eva

116

have to go into that? Just because Margo had fallen on her face with the Great Roger Munson didn't mean Eva had to put Pete down. But when Margo saw Pete, she had to admit he looked pretty seedy. He was carrying his racket and dressed for tennis in his usual ripped T-shirt, frayed shorts and mismatched socks. His wild red hair looked combed, but barely. Still, he was grinning and he acted so glad to see her, Margo had to grin back.

"Tennis anyone?" He threw an imaginary ball in the air and swung his racket back as if to serve. *Craaack*. His racket whacked against the mailboxes. Old Miss Baxter looked up from her perennial post behind the front desk and glared.

"She did it." Pete pointed to Margo.

Margo giggled. "What are you doing here anyway, Pete?" she asked as they scooted around the corner out of sight from Miss Baxter.

"When I heard at the Club that Miss Frye was away, I thought you might like to play some pro-level tennis for a change."

Pete was somehow irresistible. He looked just like a little redheaded bantam rooster with a bantam rooster's cocky, appealing way about him. Why not play tennis with Pete? He had asked Margo and Miss Frye to play mixed doubles at the Club a couple of times, but Miss Frye had always refused, saying Margo needed practice on her singles game. Eventually, he had stopped asking. Now there was no reason not to play. Besides, tennis certainly beat trekking from store to store with Cricket and Stretch all day.

"That sounds great."

"The only thing is, Allie, we'll have to play here

on the Haywood courts. As you know, male chauvinism reigns supreme at Greenbrook until noon."

Two courts were being used by Haywood parents, but the other two courts were free. Pete started out by clowning and hacking around as if Margo were a pushover. But thanks to Miss Frye and all her practice, Margo's game was sharp now, better than it had ever been, and all of a sudden, she was ahead, 4-2. When she broke Pete's serve for the second time and pulled ahead, 5-2, it must have dawned on him that she was in a position to win. He immediately began to play more carefully and thought out his shots instead of just hitting them haphazardly. He won the next three games easily, tying the score at 5-5.

By now the other players had left, which allowed Margo and Pete the space and quiet to concentrate without stray balls rolling into their court or distracting conversations going on around them. They were just about to begin the critical eleventh game when Margo saw a familiar figure a hundred feet or so away down the driveway. It was Miss Durrett. She was riding a huge tricycle, the kind old people in California used. It had three wheels and was so shiny new the rays of the sun sparkled off the spokes. Though it wasn't more than a slight incline up the driveway, Miss Durrett seemed to be making a tremendous effort and her face was flushed with the exertion. Because Pete's back was to the driveway, he couldn't see her, but Margo was so mesmerized by the sight, she lost the next game without winning a point.

As they changed courts, Pete tapped Margo on the behind with his racket. "Hey, you went off into left field on that game. What happened?"

Margo brought herself back to the tennis with difficulty. "Nothing. Just watch me steam you off the court on this next one."

As Margo walked back to the baseline, she glanced down the driveway. Miss Durrett was wearing slacks today, but even so, it was obvious her legs were very crippled. Now she was approaching the fork in the driveway. The left fork led out to the back school exit, the right fork headed up to the tennis courts. Turn left, Margo willed her, turn left. It didn't work. Slowly, laboriously, Miss Durrett turned right toward the courts. Just the sight of her narrow, thin face and outsized glasses started Margo's heart pounding. It wasn't fair. This was Saturday. Margo had to suffer all week with Miss Durrett and on Saturday she shouldn't even have to know Miss Durrett existed.

"Hey, Allie, are you going to play or not?" Pete shouted from across the net.

Margo saw Miss Durrett's head look up at the sound of her name and Margo knew Miss Durrett had seen her. She turned around quickly and though she sensed Miss Durrett behind her, she forced herself to play the whole game without looking around once. Not that the game was very long. Pete beat her in straight points, which won him the set, 7-5. It was infuriating. Miss Durrett could defeat her even out here on Margo's own turf.

"Good morning, Allinger." It was Miss Durrett's hoarse voice right behind the fence.

This time Margo turned around. Miss Durrett had parked her tricycle on the grass and was supporting herself on it.

"Good morning, Miss Durrett."

"Don't let me bother you. I'm just admiring your fine game."

Margo would have to be stupid not to pick up the sarcastic edge to Miss Durrett's voice. Pete, on the other side of the net, couldn't hear, but Margo could tell by his puzzled expression that he was aware of something going on. Margo warmed to him. He had come all the way over here to play tennis and had saved her from a lonely Saturday. The sun was out. The leaves sparkled red and gold. High white clouds puffed overhead. Margo wasn't going to let Miss Durrett ruin either her day or Pete's.

"Thank you, Miss Durrett." Margo's voice was firm. "Your serve, Pete." She crouched low to receive Pete's powerhouse serve.

Margo wouldn't have thought it possible, but by an almost physical act of willpower, she was able to ignore Miss Durrett standing there watching, and she played her best. The score went back and forth, she and Pete each winning their serve until finally Pete was ahead by one crucial game, 5-4. As they changed courts on the odd game, Margo happened to glance at Miss Durrett still braced on her tricycle. Usually her face was set in a haughty little smile with her chin pointed up, but now her face was slack and Margo noticed the long lines that curved around both sides of her mouth. Her eyes were unfocused behind her glasses as if she were a million miles away and her unguarded expression was wistful. Then, with the same preoccupied look in her eyes, she turned her tricycle around and, with obvious effort, climbed on and pushed off.

For some reason Margo looked down at her own tan legs. They weren't great like Eva's, but they were straight and strong. A funny, soggy feeling swelled inside her, filling her with a terrible sadness. This was Miss Durrett's Saturday, pedalling around this dreary boarding school campus on a tricycle with nothing in her future but more of the same. Every step, every movement seemed to be a struggle. As Margo watched Miss Durrett turn at the fork in the driveway, she saw her face in profile. It was pinched and taut as if she were in pain. Margo had never thought about it before, but now she wondered if maybe Miss Durrett weren't in pain all the time.

"Who was that?" Pete called from his side of the court.

Yesterday Margo might have answered with any one of the names she had been calling Miss Durrett for the past months, like the The Hag of Haywood or Beverly the Bitch or Despicable Durrett. Now she just shook her head.

"No one, just an English teacher," she replied as she picked up a ball and tapped it over the net for Pete to serve.

seventeen

Margo and Pete ended up having a great day. Pete was such a clown it was impossible not to have fun with him. After four sets of tennis, one of which Margo was sure he let her win, he leapt over the net, tripped and fell, jumped up and started prancing around the court belting out "Singin' in the Rain" like Gene Kelly in the old TV movie. Margo cracked up so completely that she forgot all about Miss Durrett and never thought about her again the whole day.

Pete had worked up a real sweat playing, so the two of them sneaked down to the girls' gym and Margo stood guard while Pete took a shower and changed. Afterwards they walked uptown to Hamburger Haven for lunch and Margo watched Pete devour three cheeseburgers and a milkshake.

"You know, away from Frye-Bee, you're not a bad kid," Pete said between mouthfuls.

"If it weren't for Frye-Bee, I wouldn't have been able to beat you that last set," Margo kidded back. Maybe it was because Pete was short and sort of funny looking, with his red hair that never stayed down no matter how much he wet it, that made Margo feel comfortable with him. Just looking at his cheerful face lifted her spirits. It wasn't that she could flirt and be witty with him the way Eva and B.J. were with Scott and Gavin, but at least she could be herself and joke around in a relaxed way.

"Of course, you know in reality I'm left-handed and I just played right-handed today to make you look good," Pete retorted. "Next time I'll play left-handed and wipe you off the court."

Margo slurped up the rest of her coke, took another straw from the container, ripped the paper end off and blew it at Pete, hitting him on the cheek. He laughed and immediately put a pickle on his spoon and shot it across the table.

She wiped the sticky mess off her arm and held up her hand Indian-style. "Truce."

Pete looked suddenly serious. "You know, Allie, Miss Frye is okay as a tennis coach during the week, but that doesn't mean you have to spend every Saturday with her too." He looked down at his plate and pushed some leftover cole slaw around with his fork. "You know what I mean. There's talk about Miss Frye."

No, Margo didn't know there was talk about Miss

Frye and she didn't want to hear it. Eva and B.J. were great and the three of them were best friends and all that, but Miss Frye was special. She was what kept Margo on her feet and functioning at Haywood. Margo remembered the day Miss Frye had been angry at her. It had left her all hollow and empty inside. Without Miss Frye, Margo would just fade away into the zero Miss Durrett wanted her to be. "Miss Frye has been terrific, so don't ever put her down to me, Pete."

"I'm not putting her down, honest. It's just maybe you ought to know more about her . . . I mean, that she, well . . . just play it cool, you know?"

For the first time since Margo had known him, Pete looked embarrassed, and all of a sudden, she felt a rush of sympathy toward him. Despite all his cocky ways, they were alike in a lot of ways. Pete wasn't as sure of himself as he made out. And Margo had met his older brother, Johnny. Johnny was six feet tall, handsome, and an honor student at Cornell and Miss Frye had said he was going to medical school next year. Johnny was a lot of things that Margo knew would be hard for Pete or anyone else to live up to.

"Hey, let's you and me get together tomorrow," she suggested, surprising even herself. "Maybe we could play some more tennis, then go into Philadelphia and see a movie or something."

Pete reached across the table and put his freckled hand over Margo's. His grin involved his whole face, even his ears. "That's the best idea I've heard all week."

The Indian summer weather lasted through Sunday and Margo and Pete ended up playing tennis most of the morning. Then, of all crazy things, they rowed all afternoon on the Schuylkill River. They finished up the weekend at Pete's house with a pizza. It was one of the most fun days Margo had spent since she'd arrived at Haywood.

Sunday night the weather changed and Monday was bleak and miserable, with a biting north wind. When Margo arrived at tennis practice, the leaves were scuttering across the courts and the air felt raw and cold enough for snow. It was their last week of tennis and maybe that was why Miss Frye pulled out all the stops on their practice. Though they had only one more school match to play, she must have wanted to end the season with a flourish.

First the team had to run the distance to the front school gates and back three times, followed by push-ups and killing exercises for half an hour. The worst was yet to come. After they had finished their exercises, Miss Frye lined the team up against the fence in order of their ranking and took them out on the court one at a time. She began with Trish, hit a few balls with her, and then started to imitate Trish's game. Only she exaggerated Trish's faults to such a degree that she had the whole team laughing in spite of themselves. Though Trish laughed too, Margo saw her blink hard and look down in embarrassment when Miss Frye swung with all her might and missed an overhead shot just the way Trish had in her last match.

Miss Frye moved on to Izzy, running around the

court in a caricature of Izzy avoiding her backhand. Though Miss Frye was laughing and enjoying herself and the team was laughing too, Margo squirmed inwardly.

And she squirmed even more when Miss Frye got her out on the court and began to imitate her game. Margo had seen videotapes of herself playing a couple of times and she had to admit that Miss Frye had her game down perfectly, even to the little hop she took when she served. But it was when Miss Frye came to net that she started everyone really chuckling. She exaggerated all of Margo's awkward volley shots, the way she swung too much, the way she chopped her backhand. Margo forced herself to laugh with the others, but in her heart she knew she was better than that. Miss Frye was mimicking her game the way it had been last September, before Margo had improved. Despite the chilling wind, Margo was hot and her face was burning as she left the court and Phoebe walked out for her turn.

When Miss Frye had taken every member of the team out on the court and mocked her weaknesses, she finished up the practice by having them play hard for half an hour, then running the length of the driveway three more times. When they were done, they all collapsed on the grass, panting and groaning with exhaustion. Miss Frye stood over them, looking down at their inert bodies.

"Okay, my lovelies, that's all for today. We'll have only a light practice tomorrow, but I expect every one of you to be in top form on Wednesday for our last match." Miss Frye smiled. Usually her smile lit up her whole face, but this smile never even reached her eyes.

As Margo watched Miss Frye walk down the driveway to her jeep, she realized that despite all her kidding around today, Miss Frye was in a rotten mood. It was probably just Margo's paranoid nature, but somehow she sensed that the anger was directed at her. Without even thinking what she was going to say, Margo jumped up and followed Miss Frye down the driveway. She ran around to the driver's side just as Miss Frye started up the motor.

"Miss Frye . . . I'm sorry I didn't play very well today, but I'll do better at the match, I promise . . ."

Miss Frye glanced at Margo, then stared straight ahead out her windshield. "I would have thought with all the playing you did over the weekend, your game would have been better."

How had Miss Frye heard about Pete and her playing tennis? "Pete and I only played for a little while. It was fun, I guess, but he fools around so much it wasn't very good practice." Margo didn't know what made her say that. She and Pete had played well-fought matches both Saturday and Sunday.

"Pete Montgomery is a show-off and a bumbler. You'll ruin your game playing with him."

"But . . . but he's coming over on Sunday to help me with my net game . . ."

"Fine. Whatever you want."

But Miss Frye didn't sound as if she thought it was fine. She sounded annoyed as she shifted the jeep into reverse and began to back up. Margo jumped out of her way as she took off down the driveway and out

127

toward the rear exit. Miss Frye barely braked before pulling out onto Terrill Road. A driver coming in the opposite direction screeched on his brakes, then blasted his horn. But Miss Frye didn't even slow down. She just roared off down the street as if she couldn't get away fast enough.

eighteen

That night Eva and B.J. started in on Margo about the Haywood dance the weekend before Thanksgiving. Eva wanted to set her up with a blind date, Scott's cousin Neil Lupton from Virginia. No thanks, Margo told her, she'd been through that before and it hadn't exactly been a howling success.

Neil wouldn't be like Roger, Eva insisted. Roger already had someone he liked back home but Neil had heard all about Margo and wanted to meet her. He was blue-eyed and handsome, with shoulders a mile wide; plus he was captain of his tennis team, and so into tennis it was all he talked about. Not only

129

that, but Scott was bringing some beer and maybe some pot and they'd have their own private party during the dance in the Lower School library. They had done it before and it was a blast. The thing was, though, they really had to have three couples so they could take turns standing guard. That meant Margo just had to come.

Margo could just picture handsome Neil with his blue eyes always looking over her shoulder scouting the other girls. As to the beer and pot party, she'd be happy to sit that one out. Thanks, tennis player or no tennis player, she'd pass.

Margo's refusal really irritated Eva. She hardly spoke to Margo the rest of the evening. Then the next morning, she and B.J. were at Margo again to go to the dance with the incomparable Neil. But Margo was adamant and stuck by her guns. Even when Eva accused her of being too uptight, cutting herself off from normal fun and even ruining her life, Margo refused. When Eva realized she wasn't getting anywhere, she clammed up and didn't speak to Margo the whole time they were cleaning their room.

The rest of the day didn't turn out to be memorable either. When Margo came out of Seventh period Math, Phoebe was standing by the door as if she had been waiting for her. Though Margo offered a tentative "hi," Phoebe didn't bother with the amenities.

"Hey, none of us needs a practice like yesterday's. Cool it with that redheaded boy friend of yours, will you?" Phoebe's faded suntan had left her skin sallow, but now two crimson circles of anger brightened her cheeks.

Before Margo could reply, Phoebe was gone. Margo stared after her. She couldn't imagine what in the world Phoebe meant. And yet . . . yet . . . in a way she did. Though Miss Frye hadn't singled her out yesterday, Margo had sensed Miss Frye had been angry at her, not the team. Somehow it all had to do with Pete. Margo remembered the day Miss Frye had come back from doing errands and how put out she was to find Pete and her playing singles . . . and how Miss Frye never wanted to play doubles with Pete . . .

Eva and B.J. were mad at her. Miss Frye was mad at her. Now, obviously, the whole tennis team was mad at her, too. Miss Durrett must have realized how distracted Margo was as soon as she walked into class because right away she struck. Even before the class had settled down after the buzzer, she called on Margo to read Shakespeare's fifth sonnet aloud and analyze the rhyme pattern.

For some reason, the only face in the room Margo saw was Cricket's. Cricket was blinking her eyes fast in that nervous way of hers, and she half rose out of her seat as if to come to Margo's rescue. But there was nothing Cricket could do. All of a sudden Margo felt the whole room close in on her, the walls, the ceiling, the floor. She had to get out! She jumped up from her chair and ran from the room, raced for the stairs and thudded down them two at a time. She threw open the fire exit door and started up the driveway at full speed. It was cold out and she didn't have her coat or books or anything else. All she knew was she had to reach the safety of her own room. Big Hall was empty. Even Miss Baxter wasn't at her usual post. Margo tore up the two flights of stairs, fled down the hall, and yanked open her door.

She was safe. She shut the door and collapsed against it, panting and breathless. The afternoon sun streamed through the yellow curtains and across the two beds with their matching yellow bedspreads. Even on a cold day like this, the room looked warm and sunny. And neat. Like Eva. Eva always insisted that their room be spotlessly neat. Not like B.J.'s. B.J.'s room was a disaster, with clothes and books and papers all over, dirty laundry shoved under the unmade bed, no curtains at the windows and always smelling slightly of horse.

Margo remembered that someone had once said Eva and B.J. didn't room together because Eva couldn't stand B.J.'s chaos. That was probably true. Everything about Eva's life was under control, her clothes, her figure, her hair, her makeup, her room. Not like Margo's life. Margo's life was completely out of control. Well, Eva and B.J. could find another roommate, one who was pretty and popular and clever, and one who loved blind dates. Margo was finished with the whole scene, even tennis. If Phoebe wanted to play third singles so badly, let her play it. Above all, Margo was finished with being pushed around by Miss Durrett just because Miss Durrett had had polio a hundred years ago and hated Margo's guts because she had two strong legs.

She would get out of here, that was what she'd do. She'd pack her things and leave for Suzanne's. Suzanne and Don would know what to do. They'd take care of her. Margo pulled open her bureau drawers and started throwing things on her bed. It was then that she saw it, half-hidden under some socks, the sweater Mom had knit for her. Margo took it out and held it up. It was a crazy striped sweater with all the Haywood uniform colors in it so that Margo could wear it with any of her uniforms. At the time, Mom hadn't known that uniforms were required only on Fridays and on special occasions. Margo had forgotten all about the sweater and had never worn it.

Hot tears prickled at the back of her eyes when she remembered how proud her mother had been to give it to her. Mom didn't like to knit so Margo knew it had been a big effort. Margo had been all excited about coming to Haywood back then. She would be a new girl among the other new girls, and they'd have midnight pizza parties and take trips into Philadelphia together and she'd be friends with the whole tennis team.

And none of it had come true. Margo sank down on the bed and buried her face in the sweater. The wool was scratchy and still smelled faintly of Mom's cologne. The familiar fragrance was too much. The tears welled up and started down Margo's face. If only she could have gone with Mom and Dad . . . if only she could talk to them, ask their advice . . . let them take over . . . Margo flopped over on her stomach and wept for all the things that could have been and weren't. She cried and cried until she couldn't cry any more.

She must have fallen asleep because all of a sudden, she was dimly aware that late afternoon shadows were stretching across the bed and the door was slowly opening. Drowsy with sleep, she assumed it was Eva coming in from play rehearsal.

And then her bed sagged as someone sat down beside her. She felt a hand on her back, rubbing across her shoulders. In that limbo state of neither awake nor asleep, Margo felt the hand move back and forth, up and down and it was reassuring. It was the way Grammie Allinger used to rub her back years ago when she was sick. Margo was drifting further into sleep when a soft voice began to speak.

"When I heard what happened in Beverly Durrett's class today, I knew I had to find you and tell you I'm sorry." It was Miss Frye's faraway voice, gentle and soothing. She was apologizing for something, but in Margo's sleepy detachment, she didn't know what. All she knew was how comforting Miss Frye's hand was as it tickled up and down her arms and into her hair. She didn't ever want to wake up.

"It was stupid of me to behave so childishly at practice yesterday, Allie, but over the weekend I had to make a decision to put my father in a nursing home and I've been terribly upset. Still, I had no right to take it out on you . . . and the rest of the team." The hand went on gently rubbing, almost in rhythm with the musical voice.

Margo hardly heard the words. Everything was all right. Miss Frye would take care of her.

"When you didn't show up for practice and I finally found out how Beverly Durrett has been harassing you all fall, I went to Mrs. Singleton and had you transferred into Rose Hatcher's Eighth period English class."

134

Margo's eyes were still closed but now she was awake, fully awake. She had never told Miss Frye about her problems in class with Miss Durrett. She hadn't dared. If Miss Frye knew, she was sure to think Margo was silly and stupid and Margo couldn't bear to have Miss Frye think that of her. Now Miss Frye knew. Not only did she not think Margo was stupid, but she had done something about it. And because Margo had had no part in the decision, the responsibility had been taken out of her hands. Margo jumped up, threw her arms around Miss Frye and hugged her.

"Oh Miss Frye, that's wonderful. How can I thank you?"

"You don't have to thank me. I should have realized . . ."

Miss Frye never finished. The door behind her opened with a bang and Eva stood in the doorway. She was still in costume from play rehearsal and her face was heavily made up. Maybe that was what made her expression look so startled and her blue eyes more bulgy than usual.

"Eva, wait until you hear what Miss Frye has done."

Margo felt Miss Frye tense up and pull away. She jumped up from the bed and smiled at Eva. "Hello there, Eva. I was just telling Allie that I had her transferred into a different English class. She's had a rough couple of months." All the time Miss Frye was talking, she was backing away from the bed.

With a scowl, Eva stepped into the room, took off her coat and hung it up in the closet. "I'm sure she has." Eva sneered the words as if she weren't even speaking to a teacher. Without looking at either Margo or Miss Frye, she picked up the jar of cleansing cream from her bureau and headed for the bathroom. She closed the door behind her with a firm click.

"I guess I'll go now, Allie. I'll see you tomorrow for our last match?" Miss Frye acted flustered and nervous as she edged over to the door and opened it. And her quick smile wasn't very convincing either as she slipped out without waiting for Margo's answer.

The minute she was gone, Eva stormed out of the bathroom. "Are you out of your cotton-picking mind?" she demanded.

"What do you mean?"

"What kind of games are you playing in my room? *My* room!" Eva's face radiated fury through a greasy mixture of makeup and cleansing cream.

"I . . . I don't know wh-what you mean." Margo was so dumbfounded that she stuttered.

"Are you really as stupid as you seem or are you just putting on an act? That woman is gay. Get it? A lesbian." Eva's temper was usually under control but now she was shouting. "Why do you think B.J. and I are always trying to fix you up with dates? We've been trying to help you salvage your reputation. And ours. Now I'm beginning to think you don't want help." Eva's pale blue eyes rimmed with smeared mascara practically blazed as she stalked back into the bathroom and slammed the door behind her.

nineteen

It wasn't possible that Miss Frye was a lesbian. A lesbian! She had never said or done anything except to comfort Margo when she was upset, the way Grammie Allinger used to when Margo was little. Miss Frye couldn't be a lesbian. Margo counted on her for everything—understanding, companionship, fun. Eva was just mad because Margo wouldn't go to the stupid dance with Neil-whatever-his-name was. And Eva was in a bad mood because she'd lost the election for Drama Club president the day before and had lashed out at the first person who had come along, who unfortunately happened to be Miss Frye.

That was all there was to it, Margo told herself. *All.*

The only good thing to come out of the incident was that Margo was finished with Miss Durrett forever. At least that was what she thought. But the very day she was to start English with Mrs. Hatcher, she and Cricket and Stretch came out of breakfast to find Miss Durrett braced on her canes waiting by the dining room doors. She signaled to Margo with a nod that she wanted to speak to her. Cricket and Stretch kept on going, but Margo noticed they stopped by the mailboxes so they were out of sight but not earshot.

"Good morning, Allinger, how are you?"

"Fine, thank you."

"I just wanted to say it was probably a wise move to transfer out of my class. If you remember, I suggested it some time ago. However, as I'm sure you realize, by now it's too late."

Yes, Margo did realize. What Miss Durrett had done to her in English had affected all her schoolwork. She sat tongue-tied and afraid to speak in every class. Even her grades were showing the strain and she couldn't afford that. Margo stared at Miss Durrett without answering. Miss Durrett's eyebrows were arched in triumphant crescents and her mouth was turned up in a self-satisfied smile. Miss Durrett had every right to be pleased with herself. Whatever contest it was the two of them had been involved in, unspoken and undeclared, Miss Durrett was clearly the winner.

Apparently she didn't expect Margo to answer. "Well, good luck, Allinger," she said as she steadied herself on her canes and limped over to the freight elevator she always took to her fourth floor room. Margo watched her awkwardly maneuver the grill-work door open and step inside. The old-fashioned machinery whirred as the elevator slowly ascended. The last sight Margo had of Miss Durrett was of her thin legs in their heavy metal braces and her sturdy brown orthopedic shoes. Margo turned and walked toward Big Hall.

"Margo, wait for us."

Margo had forgotten about Cricket and Stretch, but now they caught up to her. But she didn't want to talk to them. She had a lot on her mind. Miss Durrett had made her face an unpleasant reality and it was something she had to think over. But there was no avoiding Cricket and Stretch. Cricket stepped to one side of her and Stretch moved to the other like a couple of bodyguards.

"Cricket and I were just talking, Margo, and we've come up with a great idea," Stretch began in her en-thusiastic way. "We'd love to have you move in with us as our roommate."

"Our room has plenty of space for a third bed or maybe we could get a double decker bunk." Cricket was all enthusiasm too. "I've slept in a double decker with my sister all my life and I miss it."

Margo was caught totally unaware. "Well . . . ah . . . I don't know . . ."

"Since Eva and B.J. are both juniors and old girls, we thought it would be more fun for you to room with us. After all, Cricket and I are the original dy-namo duo." Stretch laughed and raised her fist in a power salute.

Margo had to laugh too. Cricket and Stretch really

were nuts and no doubt about it. And they were just about the only ones in the whole school who had been friendly to her right from the beginning. But leave Eva and B.J.? Impossible. Eva and B.J. were her mentors. She'd be lost without Eva and B.J. to tell her what to do. Though Eva might be temporarily annoyed, she never stayed mad more than a day or two and before long they'd be best friends again.

But Cricket and Stretch wouldn't take no for an answer. The only way they would finally drop the subject was a promise from Margo to think it over. Then they were off on a rehash of some old Humphrey Bogart movie they'd seen on TV the night before. Margo tuned them out as she mentally replayed her conversation with Miss Durrett. Having Miss Durrett confirm out loud what Margo already knew in her heart brought the whole problem to a head. She was already dreading an oral report she had to give in Social Studies next week. She just had to do something. But what? Now that Miss Frye knew about it, maybe she'd have some advice. Margo would talk it over with her when they played tennis on Saturday.

With Greenbrook Club closed for the season, she and Miss Frye had made plans to play on indoor courts at Tennis World. It was only four blocks from school so they had arranged to meet there. Saturday was blustery, so Margo wore a down vest over her warm-up suit against the cutting wind. She took deep breaths of the cold air as she walked out the Haywood gates. It was as if she were breathing in freedom, as if she could walk out the gates any time she wanted, come and go as she pleased.

It was funny, but it was the first time Margo had been alone with Miss Frye since the afternoon Eva had walked in on them, and she felt awkward. Miss Frye must have felt as awkward as Margo. They both made polite, stilted conversation as they took off their coats and signed up for the court. Playing on the indoor courts was awkward, too. The nets along the side of the court limited play and the hard surface was tiring to run on. Even Miss Frye who was usually indefatigable, looked weary when they finished their allotted playing time.

"I have a surprise for lunch today," Miss Frye said as they climbed in her jeep. For the first time that day she grinned her old familiar grin and Margo relaxed. Everything was going to be the same after all.

Margo grinned back. "What?"

"To misquote Gertrude Stein, a surprise is a surprise is a surprise. Telling would spoil it."

The early afternoon sun always hit Miss Frye's apartment at just the right angle to brighten it. The golden light streamed in the big bay windows full of green and blooming plants, and Margo was home again.

"Why don't you shower and change while I get lunch started?" Miss Frye took both their coats, then, as she passed Margo on her way to the closet, she gripped Margo's arm and pressed it. She had done that lots of times and Margo had never thought a thing about it, but now she jumped and jerked her arm away involuntarily, regretting the gesture the moment she made it.

Immediately, Miss Frye dropped her hand and her face went smoothly blank. "Lunch will take a little time to get ready. I hope you're not too hungry." Her usually soft voice sounded strained.

"No, I'm fine. I'll just shower then, if that's okay." Margo's voice didn't sound natural either.

As soon as Margo came out of the shower, she saw the note lying in front of the bathroom door. 'I had to go to the store. I'll be right back. Virginia.'

Margo dressed and then sat down on the big queen-sized bed to put on her sneakers. It was as if the bed were wired for shock. She immediately jumped up and scooted across the room to a chair by the window. As she finished dressing, she avoided looking at the bed altogether. But that was ridiculous. She was letting her imagination run away with her. Determined to put all such disloyal thoughts out of her head, Margo brushed her hair and then began to search for fresh towels. Margo had used the only clean towel and washcloth in the bathroom and Miss Frye would need more when she showered.

The bedroom had two closets. Margo opened the first, but it was filled with clothes. There, the second closet had shelves stacked with linens. She reached up for some towels, then stopped, her arms outstretched. Something way in the back of the closet, on the floor, caught her attention. Slowly she lowered her arms and crouched down to get a better look. A pair of large brown oxford orthopedic shoes was lined up in a row of smaller shoes and sneakers. The oxfords were unmistakable. Familiar. Hated.

Margo reached in and took them out. They were Miss Durrett's and no doubt about it. And they were tucked away among Miss Frye's shoes and sneakers

as if they belonged there. Instant insight was like a
wave crashing over Margo's head. Miss Frye and
Miss Durrett. They must have lived here in this apartment together. It was true. Everything was true. Miss
Frye was a lesbian and so was Miss Durrett. That was
why Miss Durrett hated her. She was jealous of
Margo because of her friendship with Miss Frye. Jealous of *Margo*. Margo felt a scream circling in her
chest. She couldn't understand it. She didn't want to
understand it. She wouldn't understand it.

Margo threw the shoes back in the closet with a
crash and ran out into the hall. She snatched her down
vest from the closet and was about to pull open the
door when she heard the key turn in the lock. Miss
Frye was back.

"Hi, Allie." She must have noticed the vest.
"Where are you going?"

Margo couldn't look at her. "I have to leave."

"But I have two lobsters for our lunch."

Margo shook her head, still without looking at
Miss Frye.

Miss Frye set her keys and shopping bag on the
hall table. "What happened? Did you get a phone
call?"

Margo gulped before answering, actually gulped.
"No, it's nothing . . . I mean . . . I have to go."

Miss Frye looked concerned. "Don't tell me it's
nothing. I can see that something's wrong."

"It's Miss Durrett," Margo blurted out. "Miss
Durrett lived here, didn't she? I found her shoes in
your closet and . . ." She couldn't go on.

Miss Frye didn't say anything for a moment but

Margo saw her throat work up and down as she swallowed. Then she nodded. "I'll be honest with you, Allie, because I think we've had an honest relationship. Yes, Beverly Durrett did live here, but only . . ."

Margo shook her head for Miss Frye to stop. She didn't want to hear any more. As for honesty, there was nothing honest in Miss Frye's relationship with her at all. Margo grabbed the door, pulled it open and fled. She raced down the three flights of winding narrow stairs and out the door into the cold, damp, gray November afternoon.

twenty

That night Margo called Suzanne and Don in New York. Could she come visit for a couple of days? She could leave first thing in the morning and she'd only miss two days of classes which wouldn't matter because mid-term tests were over and nothing much was happening anyway. Suzanne sounded puzzled, but right away she said, fine, she and Don would love to have her.

All the bumpy, clattery way to New York, Margo stared past her pale reflection in the train window at the countryside flying by, people and houses and traffic and towns. Nothing stayed put long enough to focus on. She felt disjointed and out of focus in the same way. Margo Allinger and Miss Frye. A twosome. A pair. Was that what the whole school was talking about? She remembered that unmistakable look in Eva's eyes when Eva had walked in on Miss Frye and her. And for sure that was what Phoebe had been implying when she told Margo to cool it with Pete. Why, the whole tennis team had probably been laughing about Miss Frye and her for months. Even Pete had tried to warn her. It was as if the whole world were in on a secret that she'd heard nothing about.

On the other hand, maybe they all knew more about Margo than she knew about herself. After all, hadn't Miss Frye singled her out of the whole tennis team as being special? Maybe she *was* different ... different like Miss Frye ... different like Miss Durrett. Maybe that was why she didn't like Roger or Scott or Gavin or any of the boys all the other girls thought were so terrific. All of a sudden, Margo's mind just closed down. She couldn't think any more. She was lost, alone and frightened, and there was no one to hear her call for help. No one except Suzanne. Dear Suzanne. Margo could hardly wait to see her.

Only it didn't work out that way. As soon as Suzanne met Margo at the door, she announced she had arranged a date for Margo that night with a best friend's nephew. Margo was exhausted, drained. All she wanted was to be alone with Suzanne and Don.

"Well, honey, that puts us a little bit on the spot." Suzanne looked worried. "Don and I have had tickets for months to go to a Lincoln Center benefit performance tonight with another couple. If you went out with Jerry, Don and I would feel much better about being gone for the evening."

"That's okay, Suzanne. I'll be all right. I have a paper to write and I'll get started on that." Margo tried to sound cheerful, but she dreaded the thought of being alone when what she needed right now was family. Still, being alone beat spending another painful evening with someone she didn't know and didn't want to know.

Suzanne put on her cheerful act too. "I've met Jerry, Margo, and he's just a nice, fun kind of person, nothing overwhelming. I'm sure you'd have a good time."

Margo knew tears were close to the surface. If only everyone would stop trying to arrange her life. "Please, Suzanne, I don't want to. You and Don go ahead and I'll be fine, I promise."

The next morning Margo was already awake, just stretched out in bed staring at the ceiling, when Suzanne tiptoed into her room. Suzanne was wearing a thin robe over her nightgown and Margo could see by the light from the window that she had gained weight since Margo's last visit. Suzanne smiled when she realized Margo was looking at her.

"I'll probably end up waddling around like a big, fat duck." She laughed as she sat down on the edge of Margo's bed.

Margo moved over to make room. "Did you have fun last night?"

"It was a terrific show. But what about you? Was it deadly being here by yourself?"

"No, I did homework for a while, then watched TV."

Suzanne reached over and pushed back the hair from Margo's forehead. Her bangs had grown so long they almost fell into her eyes. "I thought you were going to get a haircut, Margo. You'd look sensational with a nice soft sweep off your face."

Margo nodded and tried to smile. "I know, Suzanne, you told me that last time I was here."

Margo loved Suzanne, but all of a sudden she realized that Suzanne lived on an alien planet. Even though she was nine years older than Margo, in some ways she was the innocent one, all wrapped up in marriage and husband and babies. As Margo thought about all the differences between them, she knew she couldn't confide in Suzanne about what was going on in her head. Right now, when the two of them were alone, was a perfect time to talk. But Margo couldn't bring herself to tell Suzanne about what had happened and how the whole school was talking about her. And it was out of the question that she could tell Suzanne about the deep down doubts and worries she had about herself. Suzanne would probably be horrified. Maybe Suzanne would be right to be horrified. Maybe everyone was right. Maybe Margo would end up like Miss Durrett, alone and ugly and hateful.

Enough! She didn't want to think about it any more. She pushed back the covers and jumped out of bed. "I'll cook breakfast," she announced. "French toast à la Allinger."

The next two days went quickly. Margo explained away her wanting to come for a visit as a simple case of homesickness. Just as on her other visit, she refused to let herself brood about Haywood, Miss Frye or anything else.

That was what made it especially hard to get up Wednesday morning back in her Haywood room. Eva and B.J. were dining room monitors for the week, so for once they were both going down to breakfast. They slumped around moaning and groaning and paid no attention to Margo which suited her fine. Because it was a rainy, gray November day that weighed down spirits, the three of them were silent as they trudged down the wide center staircase together. Margo didn't even notice Miss Frye over by the Big Hall fireplace until she heard her name called. Startled, she looked up to see Miss Frye signaling her.

Margo hesitated, not knowing what to do. Then when she realized Miss Frye was headed across the room toward her, she hurried over. Eva and B.J. kept going, and though they didn't say anything, Margo saw the look that passed between them, and she was suddenly furious at Miss Frye for showing up just when the whole school was coming down to breakfast. They would probably be the topic of conversation at every table in the dining room.

"Good morning, Allie. How are you?" Miss Frye had on her robin's egg blue sweater and slacks that just matched her eyes. Margo used to think it was a great looking outfit, but now she thought it looked ridiculously preppie.

"I'm fine, thanks." It was hard to be cordial.

"I was just having a cup of coffee in the Teachers' Room and hoped you might join me. It would give us a chance to talk."

Now everyone was racing down the stairs to get

149

into the dining room before the doors closed. Trish and Phoebe were at the very tail end of the latecomers. As they glanced over and saw Margo and Miss Frye together, Margo felt as trapped as a butterfly displayed in a box and she was livid.

"Not today, Miss Frye. I'm going to breakfast." She couldn't help sounding angry.

"We have buns and coffee in the Teachers' Room, Allie. I'm very anxious to talk to you."

Trish and Phoebe had just squeezed in before the dining room doors slammed shut. That meant Margo was too late to get breakfast and she was hungry. Since everyone had seen them together anyway, she might as well go with Miss Frye and get something to eat.

There was a coffeepot plugged in and a bakery box of buns. Margo poured herself some coffee, added lots of cream and sugar, and picked out a bun.

"Now that tennis season is over, I just wanted to say I hoped we could continue our Saturday tennis indoors." Though Miss Frye spoke in an offhand way, Margo sensed the tension behind the casual words. "You know, Allie, your game has improved so much I'm seriously considering promoting you to second singles on the spring tennis team."

Margo almost gagged on her coffee. While she wasn't the smartest girl in the school, she certainly wasn't the dumbest. If that wasn't a bribe, she had never heard one. Izzy Coward played number two and everyone knew there was no love lost between Margo and Izzy. Miss Frye probably figured Margo would be thrilled to move up to number two singles. Margo had already made an enemy of Phoebe by

150

taking over Phoebe's position at number three. She could just imagine how Izzy and the team would react to her moving up into Izzy's number two slot. She shook her head vehemently. "I'm not up to playing number two, Miss Frye, and besides, Izzy's better than I am. And Saturdays aren't going to be so good for me this winter either. My sister's having a baby and I'll be going to New York a lot."

Miss Frye refilled her coffee cup, poured in cream and stirred it around and around before she answered. "Last Saturday you left my apartment in such a hurry, we didn't have a chance to talk things over."

Margo sipped her coffee. She didn't like coffee to begin with and she had made it much too sweet, but drinking coffee saved her from having to come up with anything to say.

Her silence didn't matter. Miss Frye wasn't finished. "Whatever my relationship was with Beverly Durrett, Allie, it has nothing whatsoever to do with our friendship, yours and mine."

It wasn't fair. Miss Frye was articulate and knew how to put words together in a way Margo never could. Miss Frye had no right to put her in such an embarrassing position. Margo put down her coffee cup. "I have to go."

Miss Frye put out her hand to stop her. She was frowning and obviously upset. "Now listen to me, Margo Allinger, there is no reason we can't be friends. You know in your heart that nothing happened between us. Ever. And it never would. I can't say I didn't consider it, but I rejected long ago developing any relationship between us other than friendship."

151

It was true. Margo did know in her heart that nothing had happened between them, and for just a moment, when she recalled those sunny, fun Saturday tennis sessions and those golden Saturday afternoons of shared laughter and companionable silence, she longed to renew their friendship and lean on Miss Frye's strength again. Then she remembered the smug glance that had passed between Eva and B.J. when Miss Frye had called her name, and the way Trish and Phoebe had looked at Miss Frye and her standing together in Big Hall, and she knew she could never risk being friends with Miss Frye again.

"It just won't work, I guess." Margo had meant to speak forcefully, to end their friendship once and for all, but what came out was a squeaky little whisper that sounded as miserable as she felt.

twenty-one

Thursday of that week, Margo and Eva were busy doing homework after dinner when there was a knock on their door. When Eva called out "Come in" and the door opened, Margo was surprised to see Trish standing there. Her big frame seemed to fill the whole doorway. And she looked grim. Maybe that was what started Margo's heart pounding.

"Enter, O Great One," Eva sang out.

Trish stepped into the room. "I'd like to talk to Allinger alone."

"But Margo and B.J. and I have no secrets from each other, do we, Margo?"

Good. Whatever this was about, Margo needed Eva's support. "That's right," Margo agreed. "No secrets."

Trish shrugged. "If you don't care, I certainly don't care." Trish walked over to where Margo and Eva were seated at their desks. She seemed to loom over them as she glared down at Margo and started right in.

"It was bad enough when you took Phoebe's place at third singles and got Phoebe moved down to first doubles, Allinger," she snapped, "but Miss Frye told me today she had just about made up her mind to put you at number two singles for the spring season and drop Izzy down to number three. I just want you to know the team is officially protesting."

Margo couldn't believe what she was hearing. She had told Miss Frye not only that she wasn't ready for number two singles but that she didn't want it. Furthermore, in challenge matches, Izzy had beaten Margo three times out of five. No wonder the whole team was protesting.

"I . . . I had no idea . . ."

"I just bet. It's no secret to any of us how hard you've worked this fall to earn that position, and I don't mean working on your game. However, I'm here to tell you not ever to count on being number two on any team where I'm the captain."

"But . . ."

Trish didn't let her finish. She turned on her heel and strode from the room, slamming the door behind her.

Margo stared at the door with her mouth open like some kind of gaping goldfish. This time there was no mistaking what Trish had meant. Not only did the whole team believe that she and Miss Frye were having an affair, but they also thought Margo had deliberately fostered the affair to better herself on the team. Margo looked across her desk at Eva, desperate for reassurance.

Eva just tossed her long hair over her shoulder. "What do you care what a bunch of jocks think? You've got B.J. and me and we'll stand by you no matter what you've done." And she winked.

Winked!

"But I haven't done anything," Margo protested.

Eva turned back to her book and began to suck on a strand of hair the way she always did when she studied. "Oh sure, I know that."

But she didn't sound as if she knew it at all. "I haven't. I haven't." Margo knew she was behaving like a willful child and she also knew the more she denied it, the less convincing she sounded. But she couldn't help it. She pounded her fist on the desk. "I haven't done anything. Ever."

The bathroom door swung open and B.J. stuck her head in. "What's going on in here?"

Eva just kept on sucking her hair without looking up. "I just told Margo that no matter what she is or does, so long as it's not in *my* room, the three of us are friends, always and forever."

B.J. leaned against the doorframe in her usual loose-jointed way and pushed her glasses up into her hair. "You know Eva and me, Margo, easy come, easy go." She shrugged, put her glasses back on and strolled over to Eva's desk. "Say, Eva, can you get that fourth Math problem? I'm stumped."

B.J. leaned over Eva's desk and the two of them started discussing Math. Margo stared at B.J's blond-streaked ponytail and the neat white part in Eva's dark hair. Eva and B.J. believed she and Miss Frye were having an affair, too. Margo felt like a pane of glass shattered in a million fragments. Everybody was putting her in the same category—Miss Durrett, Trish, the tennis team, even Eva and B.J.

All of a sudden, she either had to get out or explode. Without saying a word, and forcing herself to stay calm, she got her down vest from the closet and quietly left the room. She didn't even check out with Miss Baxter at the main desk, she just left the building. As soon as she reached the driveway, she let it all out. She started running, loping at first, then picking up speed as she headed through the gates and crossed Terrill Road. Dry leaves gusted in untidy little circles and crunched underfoot as she set a steady pace for herself on the deserted sidewalks. As the cold night air filled her lungs, she began to revive.

She must have run a good forty-five minutes before she realized where she was. She had thought she was running aimlessly, but now she recognized the street where Pete Montgomery lived. She slowed down as she approached his house. Then she stopped. She stood at the end of his driveway a long time just staring at the brightly lit windows.

"Allie, is that you?"

Margo jumped. It was Pete's voice right behind her. When she turned around, she saw him standing on the sidewalk with his dog Cindy on a leash. He must have been out walking her.

"Pete, you scared me."

"It *is* you. Well, what do you know?" Pete walked toward her and when she saw his wild red hair and big grin move into the light of the overhead street lamp, the whole inner core of her relaxed and she knew she had planned on coming here all along. She stuck her hands in her pockets and took a long, satisfying breath of cold November air.

"I know why you're here. You're breaking out of the Prison on the Hill and want to run away with me, right?" Pete's energy crackled around him like visible electricity.

"It sounds like a good idea but where would we go?"

"How about New Zealand? I've always wanted to go to New Zealand."

"Perfect. Sign me up."

Pete looked at Margo for a long minute. Then he reached out and squeezed her arm. "Wait here while I take Cindy into the house. Then we can go for a walk."

He was gone for a couple of minutes and when he came out, Margo noticed his hair was wet where he had tried to comb it flat. Of all the gestures he could have made, somehow that touched her the most.

"So what's really up?" he asked as they started walking in the opposite direction from Haywood.

Suddenly all the things that had seemed so awful only an hour ago would have sounded dumb if Margo repeated them to Pete. He had warned her about Miss Frye, she remembered, but she was positive it had never occurred to him to think there was ever anything between Miss Frye and her the way everyone else did. He took her as she was without passing judgment. Margo felt good with Pete and she sensed that he felt good with her, too. And that wasn't just because they both liked to play tennis and hack around and eat onions and mustard on their hamburgers. It was more than that. She felt good with Pete because she liked his honesty and sense of fun and endless energy . . . and because, she realized, she felt a real concern for him and she was sure he felt the same kind of concern for her.

"Actually I got tired of studying and decided to take a walk over here and say hello," she answered.

It was a phony-sounding excuse and Margo was sure that Pete knew it was phony. But he didn't press her. He just reached into her pocket, took her hand and squeezed it. "So hello," he said quietly.

Margo looked at him and smiled. They were exactly the same height. It didn't matter. And it didn't matter that Pete wasn't handsome or had funny bowed legs, or where he went to school. Margo squeezed his hand in return and they walked like that, hand in hand, for a long time in silence. But Pete couldn't stand silence forever.

"Oh man, Allie, let me tell you what happened today in Physics." And he was launched on one of his long, involved stories. Margo hardly listened. Just the sound of his enthusiastic voice was enough. It lapped over her like rolling waves, buoying her up and supporting her.

Then, to Margo's surprise, when he was finished, she told him how Mrs. Betts had called on her in Social Studies that day for an oral report and she had made such a botch of it, she'd finally turned in her notes without finishing the report. "It was like I swallowed my tongue, Pete, and nothing would come out. To tell you the truth, at Haywood I'm known as the Stammering Sophomore."

Pete laughed and Margo laughed with him. Then she started to tell him about some of her experiences with Miss Durrett, making them sound like a joke. She couldn't believe what she was saying. She had never, ever talked about Miss Durrett with anyone, and here she was kidding about it just as if Miss Durrett hadn't almost wiped her out. It was funny. Telling Pete somehow reduced Miss Durrett to smaller-than-life size and Margo found it liberating, as if a terrible weight had been lifted from her.

"I did have a reason for coming to see you, Pete," Margo said quickly before Pete could start in on one of his endless stories.

He stopped short and looked at her. "What?"

"We're having a Thanksgiving dance at Haywood in two weeks and I want you to come with me."

The words were out before Margo realized she was going to say them. But once they were out, she was glad. And she had no intention of taking them back. "We could have fun, Pete. Haywood is stuffy and uptight, but some of the girls are really nice and there's a play Saturday afternoon and a big dinner before the dance, though you don't have to come to anything you don't want to."

Pete didn't say yes and he didn't say no. He just pulled his hand away, put both his hands on Margo's shoulders and turned her around so she faced him.

"I have something else to ask you," Margo said

quickly before Pete could answer.

"What's that?"

"I want you to call me Margo."

It was suddenly terribly important that Pete call her Margo. Allie was someone else. Allie was Greenbrook tennis and riding in the jeep and lunch in a sunny Victorian apartment. Margo was done with that. Forever.

Pete looked into her face a long time and Margo could tell by the way his eyes moved that he was studying her features, one by one. Then he put his arms around her, leaned forward and pressed his lips on hers. And her arms went around him and she was kissing him back.

"Margo," he said softly as he reached up and pushed the bangs back from her eyes.

"How about the dance?" Her voice was low too.

Pete kept her tucked tightly in his arms, but he leaned his head back so she could see his face. His expression was deadly serious and Margo's heart sank. He didn't want to come. He was going to say no. At that possibility, she realized how much she wanted him to say yes. And how much she wanted him to kiss her again.

"I'll come on two conditions."

"What?"

"That we'll both wear sneakers to the dance, and you, my Margo, won't dance with anyone but me." Pete's face broke into a grin like a mischievous child's. Then he kissed her again and it was a long hard kiss that parted Margo's lips and left her almost lightheaded. She drew back just far enough to answer.

"It's a deal," she whispered.

160

twenty-two

As Margo headed for Friday morning assembly, Pete was very much on her mind. They had made a tennis date for the next day and Margo was really looking forward to it. And she could hardly wait for the dance. Maybe seeing Pete and her together would stop all the stupid talk about her and Miss Frye. Margo didn't even notice Phoebe come up behind her until Phoebe grabbed her arm. For once Phoebe's brown eyes looked friendly and she was smiling. In her own good mood, Margo smiled back.

"I have something for you, Allinger," Phoebe said.

"What?"

"Here." Phoebe handed Margo the paper she was

holding. "Miss Frye wants you to make the final tennis announcements in assembly this morning. You know, all the scores for the year, win and loss record, league standings, individual rankings. The whole thing." Now Phoebe was grinning from ear to ear.

Margo shook her head. Miss Frye wouldn't do that to her. "I don't believe you."

Phoebe shrugged and pointed to the paper in Margo's hand. "So don't believe me. Everything is there she wants you to read."

At the realization the paper was in her possession, Margo tried to press it back on Phoebe. But Phoebe backed away.

"Trish is captain. It's Trish's job," Margo protested.

Phoebe was already on her way into Kurt Hall. "Trish is sick. Flu or something," she called back.

"Then Izzy has to do it. Izzy's number two on the team." Margo ran after Phoebe waving the paper.

Phoebe looked back over her shoulder. She was still smiling. "Izzy has the same flu bug as Trish." And she disappeared into the milling crowd around the assembly room doors.

Flu, my foot! Trish was perfectly fine last night when she had come into Margo's room, and Margo had seen Izzy yesterday looking fine too. Of course Miss Frye hadn't had anything to do with this. Trish and Izzy and Phoebe had set Margo up to pay her back for taking Phoebe's place at number three singles and possibly moving up to number two in the spring.

Now Margo was directly in front of Kurt Hall with everyone pushing and shoving to get in before

162

Miss Baxter closed the doors. Boring as it was, missing assembly rated an automatic two demerits that no one wanted. Dazed, Margo didn't even have the presence of mind to fight against the crush and get out. She just let herself be swept into the Hall with everyone else. Bang, the doors were shut behind her and she was inside.

Frantically, Margo looked around for Trish or Izzy but she didn't see either one of them. But she did see Phoebe up on the stage with the rest of the seniors. And there, lined up along the front of the platform, was the speakers' row of chairs, filling up now with the usual announcement people—Senior Class president, chairman of the Thanksgiving Dance, editor of the yearbook, captain of the field hockey team. Only three empty chairs were left at the end of the line. Margo had to do something. Fast.

She ran down the aisle and up the four little steps to the platform. She leaned over the row of seniors where Phoebe was sitting.

"Phoebe . . . hey, Phoebe," she hissed.

Phoebe looked up, along with everyone else.

"Phoebe, you do it. You're the senior." Margo tried to shove the paper at Phoebe.

Phoebe shook her head. "You played third singles all season, Allinger, not me." And she went back to talking to the girl next to her. Now everyone was staring. Margo turned and ran back down the stairs and up the aisle to the doors. Two girls in senior blazers stood guard in front of them.

"I have to get out of here." Margo heard the edge of hysteria in her voice.

The taller of the two girls put out her arm to bar the way. "No."

"I can't stay. I'm sick."

"You don't look sick to me, Allinger."

She was a senior and she knew Margo's name. She must be in on this. Maybe the whole senior class was in on it. A suffocating panic overwhelmed Margo, choking off her breath. Desperately, she looked around the noisy room for help, any kind of help. She spotted Eva and B.J. seated up toward the front. Eva. Eva loved to make announcements. Margo hurried down the aisle and squeezed into their row.

"Hi, Eva." Margo tried to sound casual.

Eva, who was filing her nails, looked up.

"Say, Eva, I wonder if you'd do me a favor and read this tennis announcement for me." Margo held out the hated paper.

Eva took it. "Sure, anything for a friend in distress, and you look pretty distressed." And she laughed.

Then a familiar soft voice spoke up from the teachers' section a few rows ahead of them. "I'm sorry, Eva, I don't want you to do that. I'd like Allie to make the announcement. Allie, please take your place in the speakers' row."

Miss Frye had turned around in her seat and was looking right at Margo. Margo stared at Miss Frye's innocent-looking blue eyes in horror. She had been wrong. Trish and Izzy and Phoebe hadn't set her up for this. Miss Frye had, just as Phoebe said. Margo's mouth hung open with shock as Miss Frye smiled, and then turned around so all Margo could see was her short, blond, feathery hair.

164

Eva shrugged her shoulders, handed the paper back to Margo and went on filing her nails. That was it. Margo had to do it. There was no way out.

twenty-three

Margo didn't remember getting up on the stage, but there she was, in the last chair of the speakers' row. A moment later they were all on their feet for the flag salute. The roomful of uniforms was like a restless sea of pastel flowers. Miss Durrett sat in the front row of the teachers' section, perched on the edge of her chair with her chin thrust out and that arrogant half-smile on her lips. How she must be gloating. Now she could watch Margo clutch, not only in front of her lousy little English class, but in front of the whole school.

Though Margo knew Miss Frye was sitting a couple of rows behind Miss Durrett, she couldn't bring herself to look at her. Miss Frye had betrayed her. Margo thought they had been friends, but this maneuver had nothing to do with friendship. And Miss Frye had played right into Trish and Izzy and Phoebe's hands. They must have passed word around school fast.

Numbly, Margo followed what everyone else was doing, mouthing the flag salute, "The Star-Spangled Banner" and the school song, and then sitting down for the Bible readings, which were still a Haywood tradition despite Cricket and Stretch's efforts. Now the first girl was making her announcement, poised and smiling, and though Margo could see her lips move, she didn't understand a word of it. Margo, terror-stricken beyond comprehension, was vaguely aware of the seniors behind her shifting in their chairs and tapping their feet as if they couldn't wait to finish with the preliminaries to get to her, the main event.

Then the second girl was back in her seat and the chairman of the Thanksgiving Dance stood up. It was like a countdown with Margo at ground zero. She looked over at Eva and B.J. for reassurance, but they were whispering behind their hands and not paying attention, just as if Margo weren't about to go publicly down the tubes as the morning's entertainment for the entire school. Cricket and Stretch weren't sitting far behind them. Cricket was looking at the stage with a worried expression and her eyes were blinking a mile a minute. But as soon as she realized that Margo was looking at her, she smiled and gave a V for Victory salute. She nudged Stretch and Stretch

167

grinned and gave Margo a salute too.

All of a sudden, Margo felt better, not good, but at least not totally panicked. Somehow the sight of that silly pair encouraging her, one as long-necked and gawky as a giraffe and the other like a little monkey, eased Margo's paralyzing terror. Now air was coming in and out of her lungs in a consistent way, not just in spurts and gasps. She looked down at the paper in her lap. At first she could make no sense of it. Then gradually, the letters and words took shape. Margo forced herself to read each line through, then proceed to the next.

As the girl two chairs down from Margo walked to the podium, Margo squeezed her fists so tight her fingernails bit into her palms. Although she didn't intend to, her attention was drawn like a magnet over to the teachers' section and Miss Durrett. The overhead glare shone off Miss Durrett's glasses, masking her eyes, but that contemptuous half-smile was still on her lips.

Without warning, an explosion of blinding light went off in Margo's head. She had to do it. She couldn't let Miss Durrett sit there and crow over her public humiliation. It would be Miss Durrett's ultimate victory. All these months Miss Durrett, out of hatred and misdirected jealousy, had manipulated Margo into believing that she couldn't talk in class, that she was a total failure. Miss Frye had manipulated Margo, too, and when Margo had rejected her, Miss Frye had played the same game as Miss Durrett. Only Miss Frye's game hurt more. Miss Durrett had never claimed to be Margo's friend and Miss Frye had.

168

Margo sat up straighter. She refused to let either one of them decide for her whether or not she could stand up in assembly and make a stupid announcement.

Silence in Kurt Hall. Total silence. Every head was turned toward Margo and she realized Mrs. Singleton had called her name. Without any conscious decision on her part, she stood up, walked to the podium and placed her paper on the stand. She didn't dare look out over the now-hushed audience, but she didn't have the courage to look at the paper either. She just stood there as her runaway heartbeat filled her chest. You have to do it! You can do it! The words could have come from outer space for all Margo was conscious of formulating them, but unbelievably, they registered in her brain. She forced herself to look down at the paper. The words were indecipherable.

The paper was upside down. Quickly Margo turned it around. As the audience realized what had happened, a ripple of laughter circulated around the Hall. Trying to ignore the laughter, Margo cleared her throat to begin. Nothing came out. Not a word. Determined not to panic, Margo cleared her throat again and this time her voice started working. It was hoarse, like a creaky old leather harness, but at least it was functioning. The words were meaningless as Margo read them, but after the first initial shock of hearing the sound of her own voice, they began to make some kind of sense—scores, rankings, wins, losses, and then at the end, a thank-you from the team to Miss Frye.

It was over. As Margo stumbled back to her seat, she had no idea whether the announcement had taken twenty seconds or twenty minutes. All she knew was that she had done it. Now the usual fidgeting, coughing and restless shifting resumed. There was no laughter or shocked silence or embarrassed tittering. There was only the usual boredom of Friday morning assembly. Boredom. Everyone had been bored with Margo's announcement. It was the greatest compliment Margo could have wished for.

Margo hadn't done very well. She knew that. But she'd heard other girls who weren't very good either and she had been no worse than they. Margo knew her face was flushed with pleasure but she couldn't help it. She glanced out over the audience. Stretch's head, towering above everyone else's, caught her attention right away. Both she and Cricket looked as pleased as if they'd accomplished something themselves, and at that moment, Margo realized what good friends they really were. They were a little bit off the wall, for sure, but they had never tried to manipulate her or put her in a slot like everyone else had. They had always taken her as she was. Like Pete.

Mrs. Singleton ended assembly with her usual boring little mini-lecture on some burning current issue. Then all the seniors were marching off the stage and out the now-open doors. Phoebe passed right by Margo without a word, but Margo could tell by the set of her square shoulders how angry she was that Margo hadn't fallen on her face. As soon as the seniors were gone, the rest of the school was dismissed. Cricket and Stretch ran to meet Margo.

"Man, you were terrific." Stretch acted as delighted as Margo felt. "When I saw you up there, I thought I'd flip, but you did yourself real proud, Margo. And did you see Durrett? She looks like she's been sucking lemons."

"Stretch and I were pulling for you the whole way," Cricket said.

"I know, Cricket, thanks."

Over Cricket's shoulder, Margo saw Eva and B.J. walk up the opposite aisle. "I'll be right back," Margo said as she scooted through a row of empty chairs.

"Eva, hey, Eva," she called. "Wait for me."

Eva and B.J. turned around as Margo caught up to them.

"Making announcements isn't as bad as I thought it would be." Margo tried to sound nonchalant.

Eva studied Margo from under her heavy eyelids. "Really? You looked so nervous up there I thought you were going to wet your pants."

"Yeah, Eva and I were hoping you'd be able to get through it," B.J. added as the three of them headed for the exit.

Dumbfounded, Margo could think of nothing to say. It seemed incredible that Eva and B.J. could make those comments when they knew how hard that announcement had been for her. Margo stopped and let them go on ahead. It was like a test to see if they would stop and wait for her. She watched them walk all the way up the aisle without turning around once to see where she was. At that moment, she realized they had counted on her to fail. They had wanted her to fail. If she were weak and a failure, if she were gay even, they could control her. If Margo were her own person, she wouldn't need them. Roommates. Best friends. The Three Musketeers. It wasn't true. It never had been true. The only use she was to Eva and B.J. was to keep the room clean and cover up for them, just like their last year's roommate had said.

Margo watched Eva and B.J. walk out of Kurt Hall. They never looked back. As they disappeared out the door, Margo realized that B.J. wasn't so much at fault. B.J. was lazy and a follower and it was easier for her to let Eva run her life than to have to make her own decisions. But Eva was different. Eva needed to control everything—her figure, her room, her clothes, B.J. Maybe Eva's life at home was so out of control she had to take charge where she could. All of a sudden, Margo didn't care. Let them go.

She turned back to look for Cricket and Stretch. They had already left. Instead, Miss Frye was standing behind her. But she didn't want to see Miss Frye. Then Miss Frye put out her hand for Margo to shake, and there was no avoiding her. "Congratulations, Allie, I knew you could do it if you gave yourself a chance."

What was she talking about?

Miss Frye laughed at Margo's bewildered expression. "That's what's known as cold turkey, Allie. When I heard that Trish and Izzy and Phoebe were setting you up for this, I decided to play along. I knew if you could get up and make that announcement in assembly, you could handle anything."

Miss Frye had forced Margo to make the announcement, sure that she could do it. Why, Miss Frye had more confidence in Margo than Margo had in herself. And she had been right. Though Margo hadn't thought beyond this morning and making that one announcement, now she realized that she would never again be so terrified in class. As Miss Frye said, if she could get through this, she could get through anything. Not that it would be easy, but at least now it would be possible. Trish and Izzy and Phoebe had tricked her out of spite, but Miss Frye had used their conspiracy to follow through as a friend.

"Thanks, Miss Frye."

Miss Frye gave Margo her widest, warmest smile as she turned and headed up the aisle toward the exit. Now only Miss Baxter and Margo were left and Miss Baxter was fussing and fretting for Margo to hurry so she could lock up. As Margo headed up the aisle herself, she realized a lot had happened since she had walked in forty-five minutes before. A whole lot. And Margo felt good about it. As she passed Miss Baxter, it occurred to her that Miss Baxter was probably the one to see about a request to transfer rooms. If Cricket and Stretch still wanted her as their roommate, they could have her. If they could stand her ups and downs and worries and predicaments, she could stand their chatter and nonsense.

Hey, maybe things were going to work out after all. She still had the whole tennis team to tackle, but somehow Margo knew she could work that out. And she had Pete to back her up. Yes, she and Pete were okay together. More than okay. Good. Really good.

Margo heard the doors of Kurt Hall bang shut behind her as if to say, Over-and Done-With, and when she looked up, she saw Cricket and Stretch waiting for her. She hurried to meet them.